W9-DBB-956

THE ANCHOR
OF MERCY

THE ANCHOR
OF MERCY

PIERRE Mac ORLAN

TRANSLATED FROM THE FRENCH
BY FRANCES FRENAYE

·

ILLUSTRATED BY DAVID K. STONE

PANTHEON BOOKS

THE ANCHOR
OF MERCY

1

We lived at the lower end of a street that for nearly a century had been called the Rue de Siam. My father Jean-Sébastien Morgat was a ship chandler, and our home and place of business was near the docks along the Penfeld River which, because of rumors of war, were stacked high with munition cases, barrels of gunpowder, and coils of rope woven in the workshop of the Brest penitentiary. It was the beginning of the year 1777, and I, Yves-Marie Morgat, had just turned sixteen. I was a true Breton, short and stocky, with blue eyes, brown hair, and teeth that owed their whiteness to pancakes made of good black wheat.

At five o'clock on the January evening when this story

begins, I was on my way home from the Jesuit academy whose courses in mathematics and geometry prepared boys for entrance to the six artillery schools which furnished officers to the regiments of Metz, La Fère, Strasburg, Grenoble, Besançon, Toul, and Auxerre. It was bitterly cold, and I had replaced my tricorn hat with a blue wool cap knitted by the weavers of Goulven. My nose was red, my ears were stinging, and my hands were dug deep down into my pockets as I walked briskly along toward my father's well-heated shop and the bowl of steaming soup whose aroma was already in my nostrils.

I had first to cross the poor section of the town, known as Kéravel, which lay between the Rue de Siam and the penitentiary. In winding my way through its dark, smelly alleys I was disobedient to both my father and Marianne Treviden, our old maidservant, in whose imagination these narrow passageways were peopled by devils in human guise. Marianne was not so wrong at that. The alleys were strewn with garbage and lined by cafés of ill repute, and the closeness of the penitentiary made for a danger that I was too young to appreciate. I had, besides, a certain nonchalance that I liked to think had come down to me from my mother's brother. She had died in giving me birth and he fighting for his country as a captain in the regiment of the former India Company. I kept his insignia and the cockade from his cap carefully wrapped up in a drawer; his sword, rifle, and pike hung over the fireplace in the dining room. It was, undoubtedly, the memory of this uncle that made me want to become, in spite of my humble birth, an artillery officer. I had already allied myself wholeheartedly with the "blues" in the cause of Monsieur de Gribeauval. At this time the controversy between the "reds," who stood for stick-in-

4

the-mud traditions, and the "blues," who espoused the progressive views of Monsieur de Gribeauval, had made its way down to the twenty academy students planning to enter the artillery schools.

But to tell the truth, as I ran and jumped my way among the piles of garbage that cluttered the narrow, cobblestoned alley, my mind was not at all on the subtleties of Euclidean geometry. I was intent on meeting Jean the Nightbird, a convict by profession, whom I, however, esteemed as a sculptor. Jean the Nightbird was skilled at carving and painting little wooden soldiers, with a tender fidelity to every detail of their uniforms. Already I had a collection of his miniature figures, from red-stockinged Navy Guard to fusiliers and grenadiers of the so-called Karrer regiment which was then garrisoned in our town.

It may seem surprising that a boy as carefully brought up as I should seek out the company of such a man. The fact is, however, that convicts with a record of good behavior mingled, under the eye of indulgent guards, with the local population. Most of them worked as street sweepers, but some were skilled craftsmen, and respectable people did not hesitate to make use of their cheap services.

At a corner lit by a lantern no more powerful than a bedside candle I caught sight, among the shadows, of Jean the Nightbird's familiar, gaunt figure. He gave a low whistle, and I leaped across the alley so impetuously that I fell, with my feet sliding out in front of me, into a puddle of muddy water.

"Look sharp there, Little Morgat!"

I was known as "Little Morgat" to distinguish me from "Big Morgat," my father.

"Jean the Nightbird! How goes it?"

5

"Well enough. I shook off the coppers in order to have a word with you. When old man Kilvinec comes from his island to sell fish to your father, listen to what he has to say. If he, or Pillawer the peddler, should mention a fellow called Petit-Radet, I want you to let me know. You can write it down on a piece of paper and slip it under the stone, here at the corner. But mind that nobody sees you . . . nobody, Little Morgat . . . do you understand?"

"Will you give me the ship's captain that you were carving the other day?"

"Of course, Little Morgat. And a corporal of the Castellas regiment, which will be quartered here after the Karrer regiment is disbanded."

"Why so?"

"I'll tell you in due time. But now I have to get back to 'school.' Goodbye, Little Morgat. A note under the stone, remember, and you'll have the captain and the corporal in your pocket."

With this, Jean the Nightbird melted into the night. I heard his whistle in the distance and, as if in response, a thin cry that might have come from a rat or a small bird. I put my hands back into my pockets and continued on my way home. With a few jumps I arrived at the Rue de Siam, which was being whipped by an icy east wind. From a distance I saw the sign of our shop swinging. To me it was more beautiful than a star; it marked the cozy place where a pipe-clay tureen of steaming soup was set out on the round table. I had a healthy appetite, soon I should add two new wooden figures to my collection, my school marks were good enough to satisfy my father, and the following Sunday I should wear to Mass at the still unfinished church of Saint Louis a new brown suit cut in the latest Paris style. I opened the door with an abrupt thrust of my shoulder and old Marianne, who was cutting a sugar loaf on the counter, started.

"What a boy! He curdles my blood, he does!"

I gave her a hug, twirling her around like a puppet.

"Let me go, boy!"

"Marianne, I'm hungry," I said, pointing my nose toward the kitchen. "I want soup, bread, bacon, cabbage, cider and . . . pancakes."

"No pancakes tonight."

"If I believed you I couldn't go on living."

At this moment my father walked into the shop.

"I'm number two in my class," I told him proudly.

"Good fellow! I can see you with the blue uniform and sword of an officer."

We repaired to the table, which was covered with a white cloth, and before we sat down my father said grace. I was a more devoted son than most, because I appreciated my father's intelligence and sensitivity.

"Father Munien was talking to us about the Latin poet Horace," I said to him. "Can you lend me your copy of his odes? And besides that I'd like a compass. We're laying out the plan of a fortress based on the principles of the Marquis de Vauban. Father Munien has assigned us the project of defending Brest against an invader from the north."

"Can you deal with that?" asked my father.

"Why not?"

"Next you'll be asking me for a cannon! Perhaps I should change our sign 'The Coral Anchor,' to one more representative of my son's talents. What would you say to a streamer wrapped around a grenade and bearing the words 'The Philosophical Artilleryman'?"

"I'd say you were pulling my leg."

"I wouldn't do that. And you shall have your compass."

He went on to speak of the petty events of the day. He had sold a ship's compass to Monsieur de Kergoes, a barrel of salted cod to the Peunteun brothers; Kilvinec had come in from the island of Ouessant with a giant eel . . .

The name of Kilvinec rang a bell in my memory. Hadn't Jean the Nightbird told me to report his words?

"What did Kilvinec have to say?" I enquired.

"Nothing of importance. The usual complaints. The island has been two weeks without bread because no one dared to cross the Great Current. It's the love of bread that brought him over. We gave him something to eat and he chatted for an hour with Monsieur Sheffer, the drum major of the Karrer regiment. It seems that Kilvinec used to be a drummer himself when he was a boy, and Monsieur Sheffer was pleased to meet someone so versed in his own art."

"Didn't Kilvinec tell you anything else?"

"Not that I can remember. His conversation is on the simple side . . . Marianne! Didn't I hear a mention of pancakes this morning?"

"Your son has a keen sense of smell and you have sharp ears, Master! Just give me time to change the plates."

As I rolled the pancakes in sugar between my fingers I thought back to Jean the Nightbird's request. How was I to answer? "No talk at all." That was the appropriate reply. In my mind's eye I saw him lurking in the shadows of a tumbledown house of Kéravel.

To tell the truth, the idea of slipping a note underneath

9

the stone made my heart pound with pleasurable trepidation. An air of adventure constantly wafted its way from the world outside into our little shop. How many times I had sought it among the fascinating objects that filled the shelves! It lurked in the tackle, the compasses, the astrolabes, the ship's cutlery, the powder barrels, the tins of beef, the bags of dried beans, the spice boxes decorated with the figure of a sailor smoking his long-stemmed pipe in front of a young Negress clad in a skirt of many-colored feathers. The aroma of tobacco mingled with that of coffee—a drink just beginning to win favor—pervaded the room. My father fancied the new beverage and one of our customers, Monsieur de Pinville, went so far as to compare it to the nectar of the Greek Olympus. Rumor had it that a tavern in the Seven-Saints section of the town would soon serve it as a special attraction.

Yes, to me the whole shop was alive with the spirit of adventure. At certain hours I felt it in the collection of soldiers and sailors that Jean the Nightbird had carved for me. At others, it rose like a white wraith out of the window where my father displayed a dozen glass bottles some English sailors had brought him from Plymouth. The bottles enchanted me. They were of blue Bristol glass, and the sailors had decorated them with ingenious paintings. Into these fragile vessels they slipped love letters and then dropped them overboard as they sailed by a familiar port, where the tide eventually washed them ashore. I picked the bottles up gingerly between my fingers, because I knew how highly my father valued them and how much they were admired by the towns-people.

In the same window were some small wooden boxes and carved figures that Jean the Nightbird had left with

10

my father to be sold, in order to better his lot at "school," as he called the penitentiary. Jean the Nightbird was no hardened criminal, I felt sure. He was, on the contrary, a gentle fellow with manners that often seemed to have a sort of distinction. As I said before, the best-behaved convicts were allowed to work for the town government or its contractors. They were familiar figures in the streets, and in spite of their shady pasts, no one could fail to look on them without compassion. And in order to keep their privileges they conducted themselves irreproachably. In the morning, when I threw open my window before setting out for the academy, I used to see Jean the Nightbird and three of his companions shoveling rubbish from the sidewalk into a cart. A guard, who was called Raspberry because of the color of his nose, stood watching over them with his hands behind his back and his sword between his legs. Jean the Nightbird always looked out for me, and when I appeared at the window he gave a nod which meant: "Good morning, Little Morgat. I'll be bringing you something you'll like soon."

When, with the complicity of the guard, Jean the Nightbird came to my father's shop I always managed to see him. He too seemed to me a messenger of adventure. I passed no judgment upon him, because he was, to me, a supernatural being, a character out of a book. Somewhere I got the idea that he had been sentenced to life imprisonment for having served on a ship flying the black flag of a pirate, toward the end of the reign of Louis XV. Actually neither my father nor I knew anything definite about him. It was very likely that he had been to sea, for he spoke with professional authority of everything concerned with navigation.

Even Marianne did not view Jean the Nightbird too

unfavorably, although she muttered occasionally that he was a gallows bird. At this he would put on an air of embarrassment and say protestingly: "You don't mean me, do you?"

Jean the Nightbird was not exactly my friend; he was something less concrete and more captivating: a man of apparently harmless mystery.

To come back to the end of the evening I have just described: After supper I bade my father good night and went upstairs to do my lessons. I had to translate a tedious text of Columella. I lit the kerosene lamp and sat down at the table, with my head between my hands and my elbows leaning on the book. In my own room I felt like a young prince, safe in his kingdom. On the wall hung a map of the world, which my uncle, the captain in the regiment of the India Company, had bought from the maker, on the Rue de la Harpe in Paris in 1762. In front of me was my neatly made white bed, at my right four shelves filled with books and at my left another shelf, surmounted by Jean the Nightbird's masterpiece, a man-of-war with tiny bronze cannons. Two caned chairs completed my furnishings. I took a minute off to open the window. Looking out, I saw the wind-swept waters of the Penfeld and heard the guards shouting at the inmates of the penitentiary and, farther away, the drums of the grenadiers of the Karrer regiment.

I closed the window, but in the moment I had lost all interest in the agricultural treatise of Columella. Jean the Nightbird's words were buzzing in my ears. I took a sheet of paper and printed on it the appropriate phrase: "No talk at all." After that I tried to go back to my lessons, but without success. Who was this Petit-Radet, whose name was not totally unfamiliar to me? Where had I heard of him before? Perhaps I would ask my father the next morning.

Unable to sit still in my chair, I opened the window again, admitting a gust of cold air into the room. Hastily I closed the window and poked the log that was smoldering in the oversized fireplace. I always let the fire go out before I went to bed.

Suddenly the identity of Petit-Radet flashed across my mind. Petit-Radet was a "gentleman of fortune," a pirate; I had been less than ten years old when I first heard his name. He was said to come from the island of Groix, but had sailed the seas of the New World under the black flag, with all the navies of Europe in his pursuit. His exploits had interested us only because he was a native of Brittany, for we paid little attention to happenings so far away, and all we knew about America was the rumor of impending war against England.

I was at this point in my recollections when I thought I heard footsteps in the street below. I listened intently, and my impression was confirmed. Whoever was there was treading as lightly as possible. And that meant he was trying to conceal his presence. Something struck the windowpane, causing me to start. I opened the window wide, thrust out my head, and looked down the Rue de Siam. A shadow, dimly outlined by the light of a lantern, was visible on the sidewalk. An arm was upraised in the darkness, and a small stone, with a piece of paper wrapped around it, fell at my feet. Holding it under the lamp, I read: "Little Morgat, try to give me news." The sound of stealthily running steps told me that the strange messenger was beating a retreat.

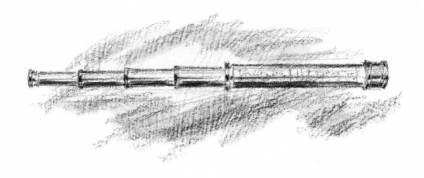

2

The academy doors opened and the students poured out, the youngest among them shouting in unison as soon as they were free to run down the street. The soldiers of the Karrer regiment enjoyed the sight as they sat straddling the rows of benches in the courtyard of their barracks, braiding and pomading their hair. They were in fatigue uniform, jackets turned inside out, with the gray cloth lining showing. They wore them this way in order to keep them clean, for the colonel had a reputation for severity. A fusilier stood guard at the gate in full dress, a blue jacket with white-braid buttonholes and a red coat with a blue collar. A corporal enveloped in a sentry's cloak, his rifle between his legs, dozed on one of the benches.

Our ears and noses were blue with cold and we admired the endurance of these Swiss soldiers.

As I came out of the academy, with my books held together by a strap under my arm, I caught sight of Nicolas de Bricheny, who was stamping his feet on the ground and blowing into his hands while he waited for me to arrive. Nicolas, the son of Nestor de Bricheny, a clerk at the naval supply depot, was my best friend. He was studying to be a painter, like Marius Fragonard whom he admired with all his impetuous heart. Nicolas was tall and blond, with a long nose; he was as quarrelsome as a guardsman and just as loyal and obliging. He went about in the evening with a sword, which was the subject of considerable comment, much to his satisfaction. For Nicolas claimed to be of noble blood and called himself the Chevalier de Bricheny, perhaps with reason, although his father bore no such title. Gay and warmhearted, he frequently fell in love, but without suffering any of the pains often associated with this condition. Between two paintings he flirted with Manon de Gwened, a waitress at the café known as "The Firebrand," a favorite haunt of officers. Through Manon we knew everything worth knowing, for she had a sharp ear and a good memory and was more alert to what was going on than a police informer. At this time Manon was, like Nicolas, seventeen years old.

Early that morning I had stopped in at "The Firebrand," which was on the Rue de Siam not far from our shop, and asked Manon to tell Nicolas to meet me as I left the academy. My father, too, frequented this café; it was there that he chatted with two of his friends: Captain Joachim Goas and Monsieur de Forster, an elderly, one-eyed, misanthropic but agreeable officer of the Karrer regiment. I knew these gentlemen through my father, just as I knew Manon through Nicolas.

Now Nicolas came to meet me, his shoulders hunched and his lips pinched tightly together. "Yves-Marie, you'd better have something worthwhile to tell me! This is no weather to keep a fellow waiting on the street."

"Come along with me! You like good tobacco, don't you? My father has given me a packet of a very fragrant brand from Puerto Rico. It was brought to him from Rotterdam by a generous skipper who, incidentally, looks like a barrel with a pigskin belt around its middle."

"In that case," said Nicolas, "you are forgiven." He pulled a small pipe with a round bowl out of his pocket and blew into it to show that it was empty.

We walked briskly to "The Coral Anchor" and went straight up to my room, where Marianne had laid a blazing fire.

"Scrape your shoes! Did you get the mud off them?" she called after us as we ran up the steep stairway leading to my little domain.

Nicolas threw himself down on my bed and asked, "Where's the tobacco?"

I tossed the packet at his head. He opened it with care and pressed the tobacco into his pipe with the gesture of a grown man and a sage.

"Well, then?" he said, after he had begun to puff.

"Do you know the name of Petit-Radet?"

"Just the way everybody else does. He's a local product of whom no one's particularly proud. When I was a child they used to threaten me with Petit-Radet as if he were the ogre with the seven marriageable daughters."

"Tell me, Nicolas, you haven't heard mention of Petit-Radet just recently, have you?"

16

"No, I haven't. I rather imagine he's long since been strung up on the gallows of Execution Dock in London. That's the tree where such birds go to perch."

"And might Manon know something about him?"

"Hold on, Little Morgat! Manon is a good girl. She wouldn't take up with a fellow of that kind. She has enough on her hands with me."

"Thanks. That's all I wanted to know."

"Tell me," said Nicolas, taking his pipe out of his mouth, "What's the meaning of all these questions?"

I hesitated for a moment and then told him about my meeting with Jean the Nightbird on the previous afternoon and the adventure of the night that followed.

"Have you given him an answer?"

"No. I'm supposed to leave the message under the stone this evening."

"Then I'll go with you. The story seems to me either absurd or else very serious. I'm well enough acquainted with Jean the Nightbird to know that he isn't one to go in for nonsense. *Ergo,* as Father Munien would say, it's a serious matter."

"Jean the Nightbird is not a bad fellow. He's known me since I was a child and wouldn't want to harm me. Mightn't he be hatching a plan to escape?"

"I was just thinking the same thing. You'd better not get involved. Did you say anything to your father?"

"I meant to, but then I thought better of it. Why upset him when I'm old enough to take care of myself? If he got wind of anything he might prevent me from seeing Jean the Nightbird again. Then it would be goodbye to my wooden soldiers."

Nicolas got up and took a wooden figure down from the shelf. "A grenadier of the regiment of Saint-Malo,"

17

he observed, turning it over in his hands. "Every detail is correct. And look at the shaping of the head! The fellow has talent."

He replaced the figure and for some minutes remained lost in thought.

"What's behind all this, I wonder?" he said abruptly. Then he picked up his hat and dusted it with his sleeve.

"I'll go with you, as I said, this evening and from there you can take me home. That way we'll be able to show that we were together. I'll come by for you after supper." And he went down the stairs singing:

Midnight is when I lock the door;
After that you'll get in no more . . .

Three hours later, toward half past nine, I put on my hat and my greatcoat to join him.

"Hurry up," said my father; "I'll wait for you to close up the shop."

"I'll be back in ten minutes," I told him.

Nicolas and I wasted no time. It was less cold than in the afternoon and there was the prospect of a gentle rain. As we walked toward Kéravel I fingered uneasily the piece of paper in my pocket. Nicolas was silent. He strode along with his head held low, so that the wind would strike his tricorn hat squarely and not blow it off his head. The night was dark and the lamps were not strong enough to dispel the shadows cast by the walls. From squat houses along the street came the voices of soldiers in their cups and the laughter of women. We came to the stone where I was to leave the message, without meeting a soul on the way. There, the sound of our footsteps aroused a discreet cough, followed by the low whistle I recognized as Jean the Nightbird's signal.

"Hello, Little Morgat" he whispered. "You're not alone."

"I'm with my friend, Nicolas de Bricheny, the painter. You know him very well."

"Of course. That's different. Step forward! You needn't put the message under the stone, because I'm here to receive it."

It is impossible to describe the lugubrious aspect of the alley, where the wind whistled as if through an organ pipe, blowing bits of garbage before it. A swinging lantern creaked above my head, threatening to go out with every gust. Rats ran over the cobblestones, making shrill cries; there were so many of them that the cats on the rooftops arched their backs in fear. I must have been unusually fearful myself, for every detail of this scene, which is a prologue to my story, remained impressed upon my memory. Even Nicolas's sword did not reassure me. He spoke first, clearing his throat in order to strengthen his voice.

"What do you want, Jean the Nightbird? Yves-Marie is in a hurry. His father is waiting for him."

"I shan't keep you long. All I want to know is whether there is any talk in the town of Petit-Radet."

"None at all," I told him. "But I don't like this secrecy. What's back of it? Tell me the truth: are you planning to escape?"

"Thanks for the compliment!" he exclaimed, laughing. "It's not so simple to break out of my school."

"Here you are, though, on the outside."

Jean the Nightbird smiled, held a finger to his lips, and inclined his head in the direction of a shadowy patch, doubtless a doorway. I glimpsed the outline of a human

19

figure, or rather I guessed at it from the gleam of a pistol barrel.

"Raspberry," Jean the Nightbird murmured.

"Are you under surveillance?"

"By the devil himself, my boy! You don't imagine we can walk out of our school the way you walk out of yours, do you? But Raspberry and I have business together. You're a good fellow, Little Morgat. If you hear anything about Petit-Radet, let me know, and I'll keep my part of the bargain. Meanwhile, have you a few pennies to give me so that I can offer my guard a drink?"

Both of us chipped in and then walked silently back to the Rue de Siam. Nicolas was sniffling. When we reached his door he held out his hand.

"Scuttle back home! Tomorrow's Sunday, and I'll see Manon at the 'Firebrand.' The sight of Jean the Nightbird and Raspberry keeping each other company in Kéravel is a haunting one, you must admit. I shall put it into a sepia drawing. Meanwhile, good night, and don't get up mixed up in any wild adventures. Look, there's your father, waiting for you on the doorstep!"

He went inside, and I ran the rest of the way down the street.

"About time!" my father exclaimed. "It's almost ten o'clock, and you haven't even started your homework. You'll cost me several pennies' worth of candles!"

I helped him close the wooden shutters which protected the door, and then we went in to drink a glass of hot punch which Marianne had prepared for our benefit. My father showed me the books Monsieur Dacé, the bookseller, had delivered to him during my absence. There were *Les lettres philosophiques* and *The Barber of Seville,* whose success in Paris was not yet a year old.

Also the seventeenth volume of Diderot's *Encyclopaedia*.

"It seems that several regiments are due to arrive on their way to the camp at Paramé," my father told me. "The sergeants of the regiment of Bayonne are in town to arrange for quarters. We must expect to have one or more soldiers staying with us."

"You can give them my room," I replied, "and set me up a bed in the dining room. I'll be perfectly comfortable there, since it's well heated."

"Just the spirit I'd expect to find in a future artillery officer! But you can sleep in my room, where you won't be interrupted in your studies."

It was the next day, Sunday, that marked the real beginning of my strange story.

I can still visualize the scene. We had finished our midday dinner, and Marianne had cleared the table. My father was savoring his coffee and speaking of my future. Everywhere there was talk of the new vigor of the army, due to the policies inaugurated by Louis XV's minister, the Duc de Choiseul. My choice among the six artillery schools was that of Metz, where my mother's brother had a jewelry shop. But above all I felt the call of adventure, and adventure at sea. Without saying so to my father, who did not wish me to risk my life in this fashion, I meant, when my diploma was in my pocket, to request service in the King's Navy. The tangent-sight and the elevating-screw, two new inventions in the field of gunnery, held no secrets for me, and I felt sure that I should win a place aboard one of the graceful frigates which maneuvered between the Pointe des Espagnols and the estuary of the Elorn River.

My eyes and ears were full of the sights and sounds of

a great naval station. I woke up to the fifes and drums of the ships anchored in front of the Castle, and while still half-asleep I heard the whistled commands to the men manning the galleys. The hammers of the carpenters and boilermakers told me that a ship was in drydock. Leaping out of bed, I threw open the window—even in the coldest weather—and feasted my eyes on the spectacle of the docks. And my imagination traveled to the open sea, the place of adventure.

My father had little patience with me when I abandoned my tedious schoolbooks in order to follow the course of a three-master, scudding with all its sails unfurled, in the direction of the channel and the ocean beyond. He would clap his hands and say, "Come, come! What are you dreaming about now, Yves-Marie?" And I would lean over my book, holding my head between my hands and trying to return from my daydreams to the solution of a problem in geometry.

This Sunday my father was still under the spell of his newly acquired volumes of philosophy. He spoke of the meager gains of the purveyors of wisdom.

"Those who sell the secrets of human dignity and human reason find few buyers," he sighed, taking a pinch of tobacco out of a china jar.

Just then the door opened and a customer walked in. He put his hands on the counter, bent his head to one side, and looked amiably at us, while my father got up to find out what he wanted. In spite of his short legs the stranger was broad shouldered and powerfully built. His face was round and cheerful and his fleshy nose was slightly split at the end, like that of a hedgehog. His brown hair, grizzled at the temples, was gathered at the back into a patent-leather case, held together by a black grosgrain ribbon. The steely glint of his eyes was somewhat contradictory to the sensual harmony of the rest of his features. His skin was deeply tanned and left no doubt that he had followed the sea. Under his dark-blue coat he wore a handsome wool suit and his tight, white stockings fitted into a pair of shoes ornamented with silver buckles.

"What will you have, sir?" my father asked him.

"My name is Jerome Burns, and I am a ship's surgeon, recently come to Brest in retirement," said the newcomer with a slight bow. "There is a second-hand telescope in your window that looks to me as if it were of a good make. May I have a look at it?"

My father opened the window and took the telescope out of its velvet-lined case. It was a magnificent instrument, signed and guaranteed by the maker, a purveyor to the Royal House. Gold letters, inscribed in a coat of arms with tiny fleurs-de-lis on the leather case, testified to this privilege. The stranger examined the telescope eagerly. He held it up to his eye and turned the screw. Then he opened the door and aimed it at the docks.

"What's the price?" he asked, and after my father had told him he said promptly, "I'll take it. It's a first-rate piece. I'd be grateful if you would have it delivered to me. I have taken lodgings in the suburb of Recouvrance, in the house of Madame Le Meur, the linen draper, next to the tower of La Motte-Tenguy."

"I'll deliver it, father," I broke in. To this day I don't know why I spoke up so promptly. The words were on my lips before I had time to think.

Mr. Jerome Burns smiled in my direction.

23

"Your son, no doubt," he said. "A fine boy."

"Yes, a good boy, but one that dreams too much of the sea."

"By George!" exclaimed Mr. Burns. (This, I discovered, was his favorite oath.) "That's very unwise, you can take the word of an old sailor for it!"

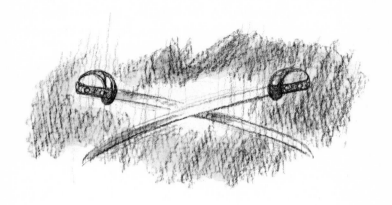

3

I was as chipper as a bird as I set out for Mr. Jerome Burns's house, the precious telescope under my arm. To shorten the distance I took the ferry in front of the Castle. It was a fine day; the weather was still cold, but the sun, shining in a cloudless sky, was a comfort to body and soul. Gadec, the ferryman, was sitting on the grass, mending a net.

"What are you up to, Little Morgat? How's your father?"

"He sends you his regards, Gadec. As for me, I'm going to deliver this parcel in Recouvrance."

"And you didn't want to go by foot, the long way around, is that it? Well, you have only to pay your fare."

He folded the net and picked up his oars, while I jumped into the boat. With a dozen strokes of the oars we were in the mainstream and alongside a navy supply ship. The sailors knew Gadec well and whistled gaily at him through their fingers. Gadec had served in the navy and he laughed back, without missing a stroke.

"Good fellows!" he exclaimed. "Quite a difference between the ways of a sailor and those of the white-tailed soldiers of the Royal Marine regiment, who are good for nothing but wasting cartridges and eating bully beef!"

Suddenly he backwatered in order to avoid a felucca that was sailing up the Penfeld with a load of coils of rope fresh from the workshop of the penitentiary.

"Damnation!" Gadec exclaimed. "There's a miserable skipper for you! He doesn't know port from starboard! More of a fool than a knave, to be sure; I ask you what he knows of navigation!" And, looking up at the mustachioed guard who was in command of the felucca, he shouted, "Port, you donkey! You're steering straight for hell!"

The guard held his right hand up to his mouth to carry his words farther and, encouraged by the convicts' servile laughter, shouted back, "Keep clear of me damn you. You'd kill your mother for a handful of pennies, I know you! Next time we meet I'll string you up on a rope in front of the whole garrison!"

Meanwhile we had slipped safely by and his last words were carried away by the breeze.

We landed at the foot of a rock covered with seaweed. I slipped my fare into Gadec's hand and started running in order to keep from feeling the cold. I ran the length of a neglected road bordered by bleak gardens, stumbling in the frozen ruts and on the loose stones as I went.

Finally I saw a gate flanked by a watchtower. A soldier of the Brest regiment was standing guard, astride a patch of withered grass. He was wrapped from head to foot in a rough hemp cloak and I could see nothing but his dripping nose.

A few low houses came into view at a turn of the road. They were freshly painted and well kept, and one of them, whose garden was carefully tended in spite of the winter weather, seemed to me the one I was looking for. I opened the gate and rapped the knocker against the front door. A woman about fifty years old, wearing the dark-brown dress and yellow-linen coif peculiar to the widows of Trégunc, opened the door halfway.

"Does Mr. Jerome Burns live here?"

Just then I heard the voice of Mr. Burns himself from the top of the stair. "The young man is a friend, Madame Le Meur. Let him come up."

I was happy to have my new acquaintance describe me in this way. Although I had barely met him he received me with the utmost cordiality at the door to his room.

"Come in, Little Morgat! That's what your friends call you, isn't it? Come in, and don't be put off by the appearance of my bachelor quarters. I envy the order and good cheer of your father's house."

"You are too kind, sir. Here is the telescope. My father instructed me to deliver it to you in person."

"Very good. It's a splendid instrument, a worthy descendant of the invention of Galileo. Just put it down on the small table. May I offer you a glass of port wine? Don't say no. A future artilleryman must know how to drink to the health of the king."

He installed me in a grandfather's chair and disappeared through a door leading, apparently, to the kitchen.

In spite of his apology the place was neat and cheerful. In the middle of the table, surrounded by books, was a monumental globe, circled by two rings bearing the signs of the zodiac and notations of longitude and latitude. On the whitewashed walls there were maps of the waters of the New World and over the mantelpiece a circular array of primitive weapons. On the mantelpiece itself, between two copper candlesticks, two shiny pistols lay in a leather case. Above a smaller table which served as a desk there were bookshelves.

Mr. Burns came back with a tray, and after pushing aside the books with the back of his hand, laid it on the table. Then he poured wine into the two glasses and held one out to me.

"To the cadets of the School of Metz!" he said, raising his glass to mine.

"But sir, how do you know that Metz is where I am hoping to go? I do believe you're a mind reader."

"No, Little Morgat, if I may call you by this appealing name. It's much simpler than that. Last Sunday, the day after my arrival, I talked with a friend of your father at the 'Firebrand.' Your father had just finished a game of chess and you and he were going away as I came in. Later his friend told me about you. You see there's no magic in my perspicacity."

"You are quite right, in any case, sir," I said. And then, emboldened by the kindly light that seemed to play over Mr. Burns's face, I confided my most secret hopes to him.

"To tell the truth, sir, I don't intend to make the Royal Artillery my career. What I want to do is to serve on the king's ships. But I haven't told my father, because he's afraid of the danger involved. Many of our friends and

29

relations have died at sea. In our town, as you can imagine, it's very common, and I understand my father's feelings even if I don't agree with them. But I must ask you not to give me away."

"I'm not a man to betray a young fellow's passion," said Mr. Burns. "You can trust me. But it may surprise you to hear that I am of the same mind as your father."

"That's a great disappointment, sir. And yet you've sailed the world over."

"I've sailed everywhere that a frigate can go. I've seen cities more brilliant and colorful than a Persian rug. I've seen cascades of pearls and sipped tea out of cups more delicate and transparent than a rose petal. Yes, Little Morgat, I could tell you no end of true stories stranger than fiction. And yet I wake up in the night with bitter memories of it all."

I sat with lowered face as I listened to this tirade. Wisdom bade me hold my tongue rather than try to argue with such an extraordinary man. Mr. Burns had a tone-less, slightly melancholy voice, but the picture he painted was as glittering as a sunset at sea, and he had a vocabulary such as to touch the heart and stimulate the imagination. As he spoke he wove a rich fabric of cities, islands, flowers, warriors, and exotic women.

I listened to him for more than two hours. And when I stepped out onto the streets of Recouvrance my head was swimming. Savannah, New England, Vera Cruz, Barbados, Pondichéry, Galveston—all these strange names were jewels in the crown of adventure. I was so excited that I ran rather than walked all the way home and entered Brest like a freighter loaded to the gunwales with high hopes and poetic visions.

At the door of "The Coral Anchor" I saw Nicolas,

who was just raising his hat to take leave of my father. I called out to him and he came to meet me. I was burning, of course, to unburden myself of the wealth of words and images with which Mr. Burns had overpowered me. I was inebriated with the wine of adventure, with the fragrance of salt water and gunpowder and exotic flowers.

"Come with me to the 'Firebrand,'" said Nicolas. "I've decorated the harpsichord of Mademoiselle Anaïs de Pinville and I have money in my pocket. I hope to paint her father's portrait and perhaps the governor's as well. I'm making my way, Yves-Marie. Before you wear a military collar I'll be a famous man. Famous in Brest, at any rate, and that's not to be sneezed at."

"I have to say a word to my father."

"Monsieur Morgat is coming too. He'll join us later."

My face was flushed and I could hardly find words with which to tell my father of the enthusiasm I felt for Mr. Burns.

"Very good," he said, trying to quiet me down. "Mr. Burns seems to me a man of quality, a species so rare that it deserves cultivation. Perhaps he'll turn up at the 'Firebrand' this evening."

I hadn't thought of this, and the idea lent wings to my feet. I ran back to Nicolas, who was waiting with his face screwed up by the cold wind.

"Let's hurry," he said. "I'm half-frozen and I can't wait to drink a bowl of punch and pinch the rosy cheeks of Manon de Gwened. We'll ask her about Petit-Radet."

I had completely forgotten the pirate and Jean the Nightbird and his guard, Raspberry. No longer did they weigh on my mind.

The "Firebrand," the favorite meeting place of officers and townspeople, faced the esplanade of Monsieur

31

d'Ajot. A troop of gardeners had recently planted trees and flowers and otherwise embellished it. Inside there was a large room with pale-gray walls and wooden panels, ornamented with gilt nets and lifelike parrots and monkeys.

From the cashier's stall, decorated with garlands of flowers, at the far end, Madame Poder, the proprietor's wife, watched with a self-assured air over the scene. Like a ship's captain she let nothing escape her attention. She was a short, dark-haired woman, some forty years old, whose charm was not in the least diminished by a prominent and authoritative nose. Her husband, a somewhat ill-humored little man, moved about among the tables, taking the customers' orders and scolding the three waitresses, Anaïs, Marion du Faouet, and Manon de Gwened.

Pipes and cigars were much in evidence; wreaths of smoke gathered and then dissolved around the three crystal chandeliers. Every group had its own table. There were the officers of the Karrer regiment, the regiment of Brest, the squadron, the Flag and Navy Guards (the Navy and Royal-Vessels regiments frequented a rival establishment, the Café Mesmin). My father had his table, and so did Monsieur Guignacet, the engineer, and Monsieur Raimond, the captain of a freighter. The right side of the room was reserved for less regular customers —a few local merchants, some Finance Ministry officials on a temporary mission and young men of the town.

My father sat down in a quiet corner to his usual game of chess and I went to join Nicolas at a table under the stairs leading to the banqueting room on the second floor. Here the darkness allowed Manon and Marion to listen to our jokes without blushing. The two girls were quick-witted and had ready answers to whatever was said to them. They circulated with the greatest of ease among gentlemen of all ages.

At this late hour of the day the room was filled to capacity and individual faces were barely distinguishable amid the blue clouds of smoke. There were the assorted sounds of dice rattling in leather cups, of friendly altercation among the players, and of the proprietor's voice, raised above the din in order to keep the service moving. When we had sat down Manon came to wait on us, gently pushing away Nicolas's hand as he attempted to chuck her under the chin.

"Two glasses of punch? Monsieur de Bricheny, you're not behaving yourself. And if you make me laugh I'll get a scolding."

"Tell me, Manon," asked Nicolas, "have you ever heard of Petit-Radet?"

"Holy Mother of God! May she protect me from him!"

"Is that all you can say?" I insisted. "You who are in the know about everything, haven't you some notion of where he is?"

"None, Little Morgat, I swear it. I remember hearing when I was very small—perhaps seven years old—that he was dead. An English ship had sent him to Davey Jones's locker—"

I stopped her short, for I had just seen Mr. Burns come into the café. Nicolas and Manon, following my eyes, turned their heads in the direction of the door.

"Mr. Burns," I said proudly, "the navy surgeon."

My father had also seen Mr. Burns and got up to greet him. He introduced him to his companions and from that day on Mr. Burns was a member of the group, whether it met at the "Firebrand" or in the back room of "The Coral Anchor."

33

Just then the creaking sound of ungreased axles, coming from the street, distracted our attention. In spite of the fact that it was Sunday, the convicts were unloading merchandise on the docks. A wagon loaded with bundles of haversacks was moving along the Esplanade. Behind it trudged half a dozen convicts, shivering in their thin hemp coats and carrying their chains over their arms. Among them we saw Jean the Nightbird, with a stocking cap pulled down over his ears. Without so much as lifting his eyes, he passed before the door that separated him from the warmth and gaiety of the café.

4

From that day on Mr. Jerome Burns was an intimate of our household. He came almost every evening to play chess with my father and on Sundays he shared our evening meal, which was the most sumptuous of the day. The two men had in common a taste for Latin poetry and for Diderot's *Encyclopaedia,* and they thoroughly enjoyed each other's company. My father had also a weakness for Rousseau, who was a subject of frequent discussions between them.

"You must forgive me, Monsieur Morgat, but on this subject I don't agree with you. Man is an animal that kills his fellows without even the excuse of feeding upon them. My professional experience and my acquaintance with so many parts of the world make me impatient with Rousseau's romantic rubbish. I may add that he himself is in no position to speak for virtues which, for all their respectability, are inaccessible to the majority of mankind."

"Come, Mr. Burns, don't pretend to be more skeptical than you are. I know that you are the best of men and I feel that your pessimistic philosophy doesn't come from the heart. You speak like someone who has seen a great deal of suffering and has himself suffered. And your attitude is willfully paradoxical."

I listened with a mixture of boredom and fascination. Ever since Mr. Burns had started coming to our house I was more and more tempted by the idea of adventure. Often I tried to reconstruct our guest's past life in my imagination. I saw him aboard a great ship and heard his booming voice cheer the wounded sailors. I tried, not always successfully, to get him to talk of his colorful past. Sometimes he fell into the trap and lapsed into a flight of vivid imagery. But eventually he came around to the same conclusion as my father's, that adventure was a dream and a dupe and that the supposedly most adventurous professions were the most disappointing.

"Adventure," he said, "is an escape valve for petty clerks and spoiled boys." With that he winked at me, while my father gravely nodded.

"But you yourself went after adventure, Mr. Burns," I said in exasperation. "You didn't stay home and rot in your native town of Saint-Malo. You left the man who had taught you the rudiments of your profession and ran away to sea. What demon—whom you now deny—impelled you?"

"There you have me, Little Morgat! I don't deny the

power of my familiar demon, as you call him. But experience has made me a wiser man. Adventure is like the carrot that makes a donkey run. But it is all an illusion. And I have come to port, at the end of my life with nothing to show for it."

However much I admired him, his arguments failed to convince me. Indeed, they only fired my imagination.

In such conversations we spent our Saturday evenings, when my father let me stay up late because I did not have to get up early on Sunday morning. Mr. Burns was always there, along with Monsieur de Pinville, Marianne, and a curious fellow known as Pillawer, who was by trade a peddler.

Pillawer was a walking encyclopaedia. He knew everything, at least everything that interested us. His wares included seed, religious books, illustrated broadsheets, cheap pictures from Strasburg and Orléans, knives, rosaries, embroidery for waistcoats, ribbons, Dutch tobacco, reproductions of military insignia, cockades, pins, needles, thread, buttons, and other sewing materials.

One of these evening gatherings has stuck particularly in my mind, because for the first time the fascination of danger entered our tranquil house.

We were sitting around the dining-room fireplace. A kerosene lamp, in which Marianne took particular pride, had replaced the usual smoking candles. It was a Cardan lamp which the head of the academy had given to my father in appreciation of a service rendered him. The company was made up of my father and Mr. Burns, both of them inveterate pipe smokers, Monsieur de Pinville, who sported a silver tobacco box, Pillawer, with a pipe whose bowl had the shape of a crab's claw, Captain Goas, Digwener, the proprietor of a boat called the *Rose-*

de-Marie, Marianne, her friend Rose Néré, the laundress, Nicolas, and myself. At intervals Marianne and Rose served us bowls of hot cider and black-wheat pancakes.

My father, Monsieur de Pinville, and Mr. Burns had been discussing the preparations for war, of which the whole town was talking. That very morning the regiment of Beauvaisis, dressed in white coats with green facings and crimson collars, the fifes and drums marching ahead, had entered the town at St. Mark's, where the magistrates had given it an official welcome. The Esplanade, where the newly planted trees were just starting to bud, was filled with spurred cavalry officers, infantry colonels, and simple soldiers, with rows of tents in chalk-marked alignment. The regiment was reported to be on its way to the camp of Paramé, where an army was being assembled to fight the English. The commander, the Marquis de Castries, was soon to come in person to Brest, to inspect the supply depots. From our house we could hear the bugles, oboes, and drums which sounded reveille every morning for the colonel in command of the regiment of dragoons of Languedoc—a big, beefy man wearing a helmet with a fur band draped around it, who was lodged in the mansion of the vice-admiral, Count d'Estaing, a few steps down the street.

Pillawer, who had peddled his wares along the coast in the dead of winter, all the way to Paramé, had a most favorable report to make on the camp's organization. According to him, war was just around the corner, and there were enough signs of it to open the eyes of the most incredulous, those whom Monsieur de Pinville defined as freethinkers.

"I believe you," said Marianne. "Yesterday the sky over the sea was blood-red, and that means something's brewing. I tell you the king's men will be under arms before the end of the year."

"And they'll die like flies," put in Rose Néré.

My father sighed and Mr. Burns shrugged his shoulders as he dipped into the jar of tobacco.

Nicolas was sitting at the table, sketching buttercups on a pad of drawing paper. Leaning over his shoulder I admired the skill of his hand. I was too young to be interested in the war and, to tell the truth, the discipline of military life had for some time caused the uniform toward which I was working to lose some of its glamour.

Marianne picked up her long-handled skillet to make some pancakes and Rose started to heat the cider. There was a movement of anticipation among those present.

"Have you heard," asked Captain Goas, rubbing his hands, "that they say on the islands that Petit-Radet is back in these waters?"

"I thought he was dead," said my father.

"Dead, Monsieur Morgat? Pirates of his stripe don't die young."

"Is he so young, then?" asked Mr. Burns. "The last time I heard his name was in 1765, at Corso-Castle, where he'd been hanged . . . in effigy, of course. He had sunk a ship from Plymouth, after plundering the cargo and making the crew walk the plank. . . . There are all too many of these dangerous fellows on the loose."

Jean the Nightbird's question came at once to my mind. Nicolas must have thought of it, too, for without ceasing to draw, he tugged at my coattails.

"Petit-Radet?" I said, looking at my father; "I've heard that name before."

"You were too young to hear it when he was sowing terror along the coast," my father answered.

39

"Yves-Marie was around four years old," said Marianne, "when Petit-Radet sank the *Couronne-de-Jésus,* just off Quéménez. For a whole week the bodies of drowned sailors drifted ashore."

"The *Couronne-de-Jésus* was under the command of Yvon Pidoux, a schoolmate of mine," said my father. "A fine brig, which belonged to the Canadi brothers, shipbuilders at Nantes. She was coming from Dunkerque, and Petit-Radet sank her under cover of fog, between Molène and Ouessant." Turning toward Mr. Burns, he continued: "You already know of the fellow's daring. The devil seemed to have him under his special protection, at least when he was operating among our islands. He had an extraordinary familiarity with the reefs and rock formations, I suppose because he was born on the island of Groix, or so I've heard tell."

"That may or may not account for it," said Monsieur de Pinville. "I've been told that he left these parts when he was twelve years old, that he went off with some gypsies. Captain Valubert, on the other hand, says that he was kidnapped when he was sixteen, on Ratcliff Highway, by King George's men, that he served in the English navy and took part in the mutiny of the *Glorious.*"

"Yes," said Pillawer, "I remember that story. It was on the lips of everyone between Lorient and Paramé for a whole winter, when the fishermen were worried about running into him off Ouessant. Then the King took over the island and had the waters around it policed. Petit-Radet faded away and no one's heard of him since. A good riddance."

"I don't understand the rumors of his return," said Mr. Burns. "What's the ground for them, Pillawer, in your opinion?"

40

"Who knows? Yesterday, at the market of Landerneau, I ran into Le Plu, the postmaster of Goayen, and we had a drink together. In the tavern there was talk of Petit-Radet. It seems that a frigate is ready to give him chase. So people were saying, but I can't swear to it."

"I understand why there's so much talk," said Mr. Burns. "The fellow has played on everyone's imagination. As an old sea dog, I can tell you that the strength of such villains lies in the terror they inspire. Once we tracked down a friend of Petit-Radet, the youngest son and black sheep of a good family, known as One-eyed Tom. He knew we were after him, and for a whole year he gave us the slip. He's dead now . . . dead as a door-nail, I can promise you that."

As he said these last words there was a cruel glint in his blue eyes, but a second later his face had the same kindly expression as before.

"Adventure, Little Morgat!" he said, clapping me on the shoulder. "Adventure on distant seas, the kind you dream about. . . . But such adventures have a way of winding up on Execution Dock or on the scaffold of Savannah. I saw a hanging once, and it taught me a lesson."

"There are adventures and adventures, Mr. Burns," I protested.

"Listen to our friend," said my father. "Experience has made him wise. Make it your aim to serve the king with honor and to win the respect of everyone you meet. Dignity and courage are all you need. Adventure is all very well in books, but in real life it's a snare and a delusion."

"Yves-Marie would find adventure in a bunch of buttercups," said Nicolas, who had just put the final touches on his drawing. He held it at arm's length, and inclining his head to one side, contemplated it with obvious satisfaction.

"Come, come; Yves-Marie knows what we're driving at," said Mr. Burns. "But I understand his feeling because, at his age, I felt the same way. Older people's sermons bored me to tears."

After that there was no more talk of Petit-Radet. The philosopher Helvetius became the subject of conversation. And at the end of the evening Pillawer sang some songs of lower Brittany or "Breiz-Izel," as we called it. Before the passage of the night watchman and his mournful cry our guests went home. They wrapped themselves in their coats and pulled their hats or caps down over their eyes while Marianne fetched a candle to light their lanterns. My father and I remained for a moment at the door to look at the lanterns as they bobbed away into the darkness, the light filtering through the cross-shaped apertures onto the pavement. In the distance we heard the night watchman calling out the hour. The thud of the waves against the rocks of Lanninon, and the northwest wind whistling down the docks made me long to pursue my dreams of adventure in my warm bed.

When I opened my window on Sunday morning I saw in the distance Jean the Nightbird and some of his fellows sweeping water out of the gutters. It had started to rain during the night and the air was milder. Some women from Plougastel, recognizable by their nunnish white coifs, were clattering down the street in their wooden shoes on the way to church. In front of Marie-Bara-du's *crêperie,* or pancake-house, some men of the Royal Marine regiment were counting their pennies before they went in. Raspberry, wearing his long sword, was supervising the labors of Jean the Nightbird and his companions.

My father had gone to the Sunday market of the Seven Saints section. As I watched the gentle April rain I reflected that in a few minutes Jean the Nightbird would be in front of our door and, under pretext of giving him a present, I should be able to take him aside and tell him the news that was burning my tongue. When I saw the sweepers' cart turn the corner I hurried downstairs and waited outside for it to arrive.

Raspberry knew our shop well, and when he greeted me I slipped a packet of tobacco into his hand, as I did every time I wanted to bargain with Jean the Nightbird for one of his sculptured figures. At once Raspberry concentrated his attention upon his other charges, and Jean the Nightbird separated himself from them. I also gave him a packet of tobacco, which he tucked into his pocket.

"Good morning, Little Morgat, and thank you. The town is full of soldiers, and there's war in the air."

"Listen, Jean the Nightbird, I have something to tell you. Petit-Radet is near by."

I spoke in a low voice, scrutinizing him in order to catch his reaction. I was not disappointed, for he turned very pale. Then he recovered his composure to some extent, scratched his nose, and said breathlessly, "How did you find out, Little Morgat?"

"From Pillawer."

"Devil take us, Little Morgat! Meet me at midnight by the stone, and I'll tell you what to do. Don't breathe it to a soul; you've nothing to fear. You'll be thanked for your good deed, even if soon, as I hope, I'm far away."

Just then Raspberry struck a wheel of the cart with his sword, and Jean the Nightbird hastened to rejoin him, whispering over his shoulder, "This evening, remember!"

I returned to my room in a state of uncommon excitement. Every word of Jean the Nightbird had made an imprint upon my imagination. I understood his way of talking, and the importance of what he had said did not escape me. Besides, I had seen the emotion betrayed by his face. Something meaningful and irresistible had been building up ever since our first secret exchange in the garbage-filled alley of Kéravel some days before. My blood ran quick in my veins and I hurried to get fully dressed and run to see Nicolas. I had sworn secrecy and I had no intention of telling him what had happened. What I wanted was to borrow his sword. I was tempted, for a moment, to ask Mr. Burns for one of the pistols I had seen on his mantelpiece. But I was wise enough to perceive the rashness of such a request.

When it came to Nicolas I would surely be able to find a pretext. He was as sharp as a fox, but at the same time very trusting. I'd tell him a cock-and-bull story of some kind. . . . I didn't know exactly what, because lying was contrary to my nature. I bit my fingers impatiently, but instead of hurrying out I bided my time. At noon I had not yet found a solution.

The solution, when it came, was provided by Nicolas himself. That afternoon I found him in the attic he pretentiously called his studio, standing in front of a large sheet of paper which he had nailed to the wall. On it he had drawn a life-size human figure with which he was shadow-fencing. His shirtsleeves were rolled up and his face was streaming with perspiration. When I walked in he threw his sword onto the floor; it struck the foot of a stool as it fell.

"I've had enough!" he exclaimed. "But it's not a bad

44

exercise, fencing, and I recommend it to you."

Immediately I fell in with this suggestion and asked him to lend me both the sword and the dummy.

"I'll see that you get them back tomorrow," I assured him. "My father or Marianne will bring them around, I promise."

When I left Nicolas's house my cheeks were flaming, and I was not particularly proud of myself. Under my arm I carried the fruit of my first lie and also an object of no small danger. I was not entitled to carry a sword, and on this point the king's ordinances were very severe.

5

The night watchman had just called out midnight when I opened my window. I had been lying on my bed, wide-awake and fully dressed, listening nervously to the slightest sounds of the sleeping house. When the watchman turned the corner I leaped to my feet and plunged my face into a basin of cold water. I fastened Nicolas's sword belt around my waist and buttoned my coat over it. Then I looked down at the street, where nothing stirred except for two cats, one running after the other along the walls. The only sound was the familiar one of the rising tide, which at this hour I found vaguely disturbing. I threw one leg over the window sill and slid, like a spider at the end of its thread, down the rain pipe. For the first time in my life I was starting out to spend the night away from home.

I had studied the operation carefully, testing the strength of the pipe and making sure that no sound would betray me. Now I landed easily at the bottom, assured that I could climb safely back to my room at dawn. I had calculated that my meeting with Jean the Nightbird might last for some hours, but I had no idea of its far-reaching consequences.

When my feet hit the ground the sudden reality of my adventure made my heart start pounding. Pausing to look to right and left, I saw no danger. Actually my only concern was that I might have awakened my father. Reassured on this point I set out, closely skirting the walls, to keep my appointment. The narrow, squat houses of Kéravel were like so many tombs in a silent cemetery.

By the time I reached the famous stone I had lost my momentary fears. The feel of the sword against my legs was a guarantee of protection. For half an hour I waited, leaning against a damp wall. The weather was mild and in the air there were signs of spring. In spite of the foul smell of the neighborhood I thought I could detect the fragrance of the flowers just beginning to bud in the Portzic gardens. Suddenly the sound of approaching footsteps caused me to finger the hilt of my sword. A moment later I heard the whistle of Jean the Nightbird and then his voice, saying, "Are you there, Little Morgat?"

I stepped out of the shadows and found both Jean the Nightbird and Raspberry before me.

"Very good," said the convict. "You're a man of your word. Follow me, and have no fear. You know by now that Raspberry is a friend. We'll go to a safe house, where you'll always find a welcome."

Raspberry raised a finger to his lips in warning. The sound of marching footsteps, first muffled then loud and clear, rang out in the night.

"A patrol," said Jean the Nightbird. "Quick, around the corner, until the coppers have gone by!"

Half a dozen constables, carrying pikes or muskets on their shoulders, and breathing heavily as they made their way among the loose cobblestones, passed within inches of where we had taken our stand. When they had gone Jean the Nightbird started to tiptoe rapidly away and we followed. In two or three minutes he stopped in front of a low door and rapped, obviously in a prearranged signal. Apparently we were expected, for the door at once swung open and then closed behind us.

We were in a tavern, empty at this hour, but where the tables were still littered with carafes and dirty dishes and there was an overpowering smell of grease and stale cider. The proprietor was a giant of a man, with eyes as round and hard as those of a falcon and on his head the red cap typical of the village of Plougastel. With the back of his hand he cleared a table, and we pulled over some stools from a pile stacked against the wall.

"Thomas the Souse," said Jean the Nightbird, pointing in his direction. "Once he's laid eyes on you you'll never be forgotten. He's a tough buzzard, but a sure friend. If ever you need him, just knock at the door of 'Neptune's Wood,' in case you didn't see the sign over the door."

Thomas the Souse (a name which seemed to indicate English origins) held out his hand. The familiarity of the gesture made me feel ill at ease, but I couldn't very well refuse to shake it.

"Give us some wine, and keep an eye on the door," said Jean the Nightbird. "We don't want to be disturbed."

"What if Ninon Glao drops in to see you?"

"Throw her out," said Jean the Nightbird roughly.

Thomas the Souse grinned from ear to ear and went to draw some wine.

"Now let's get down to business," said Jean the Nightbird, leaning his elbows on the greasy table. "First, Little Morgat, let me say that I don't want to get you in trouble. You're doing more for us than you have any idea. Next, I want you to know that Raspberry here is a partner in my little game. The stakes are high: freedom for me, and for him a fortune. You know that I wanted to find out about Petit-Radet. I had a feeling that the islander Kilvinec, or Pillawer, the peddler, would have news of him. Pillawer is a reliable source of information and I'm grateful to you for bringing me word so quickly. I hate this fellow, Petit-Radet; in fact if I am shut up in school, it's his fault. Ten years I've been waiting, ever since I came in chains from Paris. It was at Paris that they nabbed me. Petit-Radet got away, leaving me to fall into the trap that was set to catch him. But I always settle my accounts, and by God I'll settle this one! Besides, there's a price on his head, and I'll soon find out how much. Raspberry here has an account to settle with him also. If he can lay hands on him he'll split the reward with me. I can't promise you a cut, and I'm sure you'd turn it down, anyway. But I know I can count on your courage and your kind heart. The deal we're proposing isn't in any way dirty. It's a question of ridding the world of a murderer and freeing an innocent man."

I was struck dumb by this story. "What's to be done?"

"Have a drink of wine, my boy; not too much, because you're not used to it. Pull yourself together and think over what I have just told you."

49

I drank two fingers of white wine, but my hands were trembling and I had to make two attempts to raise the glass to my lips. When I put it back on the table my mind was made up.

"Jean the Nightbird, do you solemnly promise that you are innocent?"

"By the memory of my dead mother, I swear it!"

"I believe you. I'll do all I can to help. I mean all I can do with the time I have at my disposal and without worrying my father."

"You have only to watch the harbor from a point near the Castle, where we're forbidden to go. Besides, Petit-Radet knows Raspberry and myself and if he caught sight of us he'd know there was something up. Whereas if you should happen to run into him he'd have no cause for alarm."

"But how shall I recognize him?"

"We'll describe him to you. And I have in my pocket a painted wooden figure that's a perfect likeness. A spitting image, isn't it, Raspberry? It shows him in the red coat he was wearing on the bridge of his ship when he captured a couple of unlucky fellows and myself off Caracas. That was when my troubles began."

Just then there was a loud knock at the door and a woman's voice came through the keyhole. "Get out of there, get out in a hurry! There are over fifty of them, and they're going to surround the house."

"That's Ninon Glao," said Raspberry, leaping to his feet.

Her voice sounded again, in a shrill cry from the street, followed by the click of bayonets.

"Over the rooftops!" said Thomas the Souse, pointing to a stair leading up to the attic.

Before I knew it I was lying flat on my stomach, encumbered by my sword, at the base of a tall chimney. The cold night air shocked me into awareness of my plight. What a fool I was to have got myself into such a wasp's nest! Somehow I must get out of it and throw off these compromising companions. Raspberry was crouching beside me, and although I couldn't see his face I felt that he was paralyzed with fear. The same fear threatened to grip me, but I swore I wouldn't give in to it. I bit my lips and breathed deeply of the bracing air.

From where I was lying I couldn't see the street but I could hear the clamor raised by the constables and soldiers who were gathering there. The shutters of the adjoining houses were thrown open and I heard a woman screaming insults. Then there was the sound of a violent slap, a woman's sobbing, and loud masculine laughter. A door creaked immediately below. After giving us time to escape Thomas the Souse must have decided to open "Neptune's Wood" to the forces of the law.

I started to crawl away from the trembling Raspberry, and as I did so I saw that Jean the Nightbird was trying to attract our attention. I reached back and touched Raspberry's arm. Strangely enough this simple gesture freed him of his fear. He crawled after me until we reached Jean the Nightbird, on the other side of the chimney, who pointed the way among the forest of chimneys around us. "Back to the fold!" he whispered.

After crawling for some distance we slid, one after the other, down a rain pipe and landed on the broken cobblestones of a dark alley which wound its way to the east side of the penitentiary. Suddenly a cannon shot shattered the silence.

"That's it!" cried Jean the Nightbird. "The peniten-

51

tiary has given the definitive alarm. Next they'll have the bloodhounds on our trail. We must strike for the open fields. But you, Little Morgat, had better head for home. I'll find a way of getting in touch with you."

Without further word he faded away in the darkness, pulling Raspberry behind him. I was left alone under a sudden downpour of rain.

Now the problem was to get home without being seen. I proceeded cautiously, trying to think what excuse I could give for my presence on the streets if I were to run into a patrol. The whole of Kéravel seemed to have come to life; I fancied I heard footsteps and clicking bayonets in every direction. At the same time the stormy wind was toppling chimneys around me, making the confusion even greater. I was lost among a tangle of alleys when, at a corner, I heard a familiar muffled voice.

"Little Morgat!"

Turning my head I saw Jean the Nightbird, crouching like a toad behind the corner post of a carriage gateway.

"Follow me! The police have barricaded the Rue de Siam. They're arresting everyone who tries to get through, and there's no chance of your slipping by."

Tears welled up in my eyes as I foresaw the dire consequences of my unfortunate escapade. All I could do was groan, "I'm out of luck, God help me!"

"We've decided to make for Lambézellec. When we get there we'll decide what to do next. Raspberry has gone ahead."

My spirit was broken, and I nodded assent. We made our way out of Kéravel without mishap. When we reached a path through the fields Jean the Nightbird tightened his belt and ran like a lean wolf through the darkness. I followed in his footsteps, but after half an hour I was out of breath and voiced a complaint.

"We'll take it easy for a moment, Little Morgat," he said, bringing a flask out of his pocket. We both had a swig of rum.

"That will set us up," said my companion. "When we get to our destination I'll be able to change my clothes. And the way will be clear for you to go home. I'll help you find an excuse to give your father. We'll figure that out later. He can't reproach you for anything worse than having chosen a bad night to go out. The main thing is to shake our pursuers. I intend to keep my head out of the noose and my body out of jail, I can tell you!"

For two more hours we walked on. A glow in the east announced the coming of dawn.

"In another hour it won't be safe for us to show our faces," said Jean the Nightbird. "We'll hide out in those woods just ahead on our right. It will be a long day, my boy, but we'll employ it in making up a story to facilitate the return of the prodigal son."

He spoke in a humorous vein, but I was in no mood for joking. I was tired and hungry and more than a little anxious about the consequences of my great adventure. Jean the Nightbird gave me some more rum and this revived my spirits. I stopped worrying about my father's anger, the reproaches of Mr. Burns, and the dressing-down I was sure to receive from Marianne and thought, rather, of the fine story I would have to tell Nicolas.

We approached the wood cautiously. Jean the Night-bird sniffed the terrain like a wild boar searching for a wallow. Finally we sought refuge in a big oak whose branches and new leaves were thick enough to afford us protection.

"Climb up," said Jean the Nightbird, lending me his shoulder.

He climbed after me and chose a perch from which we could survey the road we had just traveled. In the distance I saw an isolated house.

"That's Ker-Gorret," he told me, "the home of an old shipmate of mine who will lend me some clothes and also give us something to eat. We'll need it, because until nightfall there's no prospect of anything but rum."

We settled down, each of us on a branch, like two crows on the look-out. Jean the Nightbird had, indeed, a nose as hooked as the beak of a crow.

As he had foretold, the day was a long one. It was still drizzling and our clothes were thoroughly soaked. Toward noon we had recourse to another swig of rum. Early in the afternoon some horsemen appeared on the road. At first they were too far away for us to distinguish their uniforms, but soon we decided that they belonged to the constabulary. Jean the Nightbird's keen eyes made out the muskets swinging from their saddles.

"They're after us, if I'm not mistaken," he said grimly. "We did well to hide in the tree. Tomorrow night we'll be safe, you in your own warm bed and I . . . somewhere or other. I'm to meet Raspberry on the coast south of here, on Sunday. Then I'll take care of Petit-Radet and return to a more normal way of living. No more adventures from now on! Take it from me, Little Morgat, you'll be well advised to study hard and win yourself a good place in the service of the king."

"You're talking like Mr. Burns."

"Then Mr. Burns, whoever he may be, has the right idea, and you'd do well to lend him an ear. But there are things that a boy of your age can't understand, and it's no use my insisting. Right now all we can do is look forward to sinking our teeth into a loaf of bread and a rasher of bacon. And what would you say to a jug of cider to wash them down?"

The idea of a square meal inspired me to be patient. We spent the rest of the afternoon making up a story for me to tell my father. I had been awakened by a clatter of arms—this was what we finally decided I should say—and had gone down to the street to see what was happening. The constables were laying hands on everyone they saw, and I had no recourse but to flee into the country. The story had some semblance of truth; indeed, there were facts to confirm it. Jean the Nightbird helped to embroider the details, and when we had finished I had less fear for the morrow.

When darkness fell we climbed down from the tree. Our legs were so stiff that it took us several minutes to get moving. Slowly, we made our way to the little house hidden behind an apple orchard and a hedge of barberry bushes. Jean the Nightbird gave his characteristic whistle, and the door was thrown open. The man who greeted us looked very much like Thomas the Souse. While we were up on the tree Jean the Nightbird had told me that he was Thomas's brother and that his name was Guénolé.

6

Guénolé was a sturdy old man. I learned later that during the great Mutiny he was sentenced to ten years on the galleys. He was one of the last convicts to serve as galley slaves. In 1754 convicts were taken off the king's galleys and Guénolé benefited by a pardon. In this year of 1777 he must have been fifty-six years old.

He gave us food and drink and, to the great joy of Jean the Nightbird, I gobbled everything up like a young puppy. "Here's a good customer for you!" he said to his old shipmate.

But Guénolé did not laugh. He was intent upon watching Jean the Nightbird pick out a sailor's uniform from the bunch of ragged clothes he had tossed onto the beaten-dirt floor. As for Jean the Nightbird, when he had clothed himself from head to foot he made a bundle of his convict garb and said, "Take this stuff out and bury it!"

Guénolé obeyed, while I finished up the bread and bacon and cider.

"Lie down on this cot, Little Morgat," said Jean the Nightbird. "When you've had a good rest you'll be in better shape to start home."

"I'd like to wash," I told him.

I was as black as a chimney sweep and my wet, muddy clothes were sticking to my skin. Jean the Nightbird brought me a bucket of water, some soap, and a towel. While I was washing he lit a log in the fireplace and hung my clothes in front of it.

"I'll brush them off when they're dry," he told me. "With this roaring blaze it won't be long."

As soon as I was clean I felt bold enough to start on my return journey. But Jean the Nightbird made his will prevail.

"You must wait for dark, Little Morgat. The roads aren't safe by day. And for my own security it's better that no one should see you leave this house. For all we know the gentlemen on horseback we saw from the tree are lying in ambush near by."

Another day was about to dawn, and this meant hours of unwelcome confinement. It seemed to me that Jean the Nightbird was overly cautious, and I was not too happy to linger in my present company. Now that the feverish excitement of the flight had subsided I could look objectively at my situation. The doubtful honesty of these jailbirds was not exactly reassuring.

I lay down on Guénolé's cot, with my hands under my

head, and reflected upon my predicament. Beside me, on a stool, was Nicolas's sword. This was the last thing I saw before falling into a dead sleep.

When I woke up I had difficulty, at first, in remembering where I was. I thought for a moment that I was in my own room, and it was hard to face the shock of reality. I rubbed my eyes and sat up, with my legs dangling over the side of the cot. The room was empty but I could hear Jean the Nightbird talking to Guénolé in the adjoining shed.

"The boy's asleep, and he won't be awake before morning. I want to keep him with me, on account of the coppers. He's not old enough to keep his mouth shut in court. We'll send him back to his father's shop when we're safely on the way to Quimper. Petit-Radet will be going there to see his lawyer. And that's when I'll have the last laugh. I'll be there, too, to settle accounts with him."

"Don't talk so loudly," Guénolé warned him. "The walls are paper-thin, and the kid may hear us."

A moment later Jean the Nightbird pushed open the door. I yawned and rubbed my eyes as if I were just waking up.

"Are you awake, Little Morgat?"

"Barely. Where have you been?"

I played innocent in order to cope with the new danger. The conversation I had just overheard was alarming, and I made up my mind to escape at the earliest opportunity.

"It's seven o'clock in the evening," said Jean the Nightbird. "We'll have a bite to eat, and then Guénolé will take us along the coast by boat, so as to avoid the coppers. It seems they're patroling the area of Lambézellec, Guilers, and Locmaria. Just now he's keeping an eye on the Kérinon road." As he spoke he put some bread and cheese on the table, cut them, and gave me some slices.

"Put these in your pocket," he said. "Toward morning you may be hungry."

He himself began to eat, stuffing huge pieces of bread into his mouth. Then he lit his pipe and went to stand by the door, listening to the sounds of the night. All of a sudden he turned to me and shouted, "Put on your sword!"

Quickly I buckled the belt around my waist.

"Did you hear?" he asked.

I shook my head.

"It's Guénolé . . . listen . . ."

I heard what sounded like the distant hoot of an owl.

"That's the all-clear signal," said Jean the Nightbird. "Now we can join him."

He wrapped himself in a shepherd's cloak and picked up a stout stick standing in a corner. The night air was mild and we could hear the sea in the distance. I hadn't realized we were so far from Brest and confided my dismay to my companion.

"It's no more than ten miles to Kéravel," he said reassuringly. "If we make good time and nothing interferes you'll be there by dawn. That's a good time to slip home without getting a scolding. Your father will be sleepy, and so glad to see you that he won't preach any sermons. But I can't let you go until it's quite safe. After all, I'm responsible for your being here."

"I want to get home."

"You're on the way, I tell you. In half an hour I'll tell you goodbye."

"Where are we, exactly?"

"About three miles from Lampaul. . . . Look out there, damn it!"

He caught me by the arm and pulled me behind a hedge.

"Lie low and don't move!" he whispered hoarsely.

I held my breath, but turning my head I saw four horsemen strung out on the road. They were riding against the wind, and for this reason we hadn't heard them. Fortunately Jean the Nightbird had a keen eye. The horsemen passed right in front of us. They were wearing the blue coats with red facings of the constabulary and their guns, instead of being slung across the saddles, were in their hands. They were riding slowly, rocked by the easy gait of their horses. One of them said, "It's not today we'll be getting the reward."

"The night isn't yet over," said one of his comrades. "We may yet see a fire. Then it will be time to speak of rewards. The wreckers are more and more bold. With those fires they light along the shore they've enticed dozens of boats onto the rocks and plundered them at leisure."

When they had disappeared from sight we extricated ourselves from the hedge. I had scratches all over my face and hands.

"You see, I was right," said Jean the Nightbird. "In a couple of hours there'll be a hundred coppers on our trail."

Just then Guénolé arrived on the scene. His muddy clothes showed that he had thrown himself down on the ground.

"Did you see?" he asked Jean the Nightbird. He paid no attention to me.

"We must get to your boat as quickly as possible. The

wind will take us to Camaret and there we'll put the boy down and let him make his own way to Brest."

"I lit three fires," said Guénolé, "but I might have done better to save the wood. In an hour the coppers will have sighted them."

"No, you did well. While they're looking for us at the site of the fires we'll embark farther along the coast. I say you had the right idea."

"That may be," said Guénolé disgruntledly. "It'll take us half an hour of running to reach the coast. If Charlot has the boat ready we can make for the open sea, avoiding the coast guard on our way. Well, we'll see how it turns out. We've done the best we can."

We ran, stumbling, toward the sea. My head was whirling. I could still hear the tread of the horses and the priming of guns. And I understood now that Guénolé was a professional wrecker. I thought of my father and Mr. Burns and the academy. The very names caused the blood to rise to my head and my cheeks and my ears to redden.

After running down a hollowed-out road bordered by gnarled trees, and crossing a moor where thistles pricked our ankles, we came to the sea. The tide was just starting to roll in and the waves roared as they broke, leaving a carpet of foam behind them. We went down onto a pebbled beach, already flooded with water. Guénolé walked ahead; suddenly he stepped around a rock and whistled through his fingers. The shrill sound could be heard over the waves.

"Charlot's waiting," he said after a moment. "We'll have to wade out up to our hips."

He led us into the waves. Suddenly a black shape loomed up ahead of us, and we hoisted ourselves aboard, soaking wet up to the necks.

"Damnation!" exclaimed Jean the Nightbird. "Now I can breathe easy."

"You'll breathe easier when we get to Camaret," said Guénolé.

I sat huddled on the bottom of the boat. I was shivering and dizzy, but I could hear the creaking of the boom and the flapping of the main jib which Charlot was hoisting. It swelled out in the breeze, and Guénolé added a flying jib to the rigging. Water lapped against the keel. The wind was favorable, and at just this moment the moon peered out from between two clouds like the bright eye of an owl in a forest clearing. In its light we glimpsed the outline of a coast-guard boat, armed with a cannon at the prow. Like all such craft it was able to sail very close to the wind, thus putting us at a distinct disadvantage. Jean the Nightbird, Guénolé, and Charlot all made wry faces. As for me, I had a sudden access of courage. Leaping to my feet I said resolutely, "Jean the Nightbird, put me ashore immediately! I don't want to stay aboard a minute longer."

"Are you mad, boy?"

"No, I'm not mad. I want to be put ashore." And I added, imprudently, "I know what I know!"

"I say that you have to stick with us," said Guénolé, for the first time addressing me directly.

With my hand on the hilt of my sword I backed up against the starboard side of the boat, resolved to fight for my rights.

Charlot stayed at the tiller while Guénolé and Jean the Nightbird consulted at the bow. The former folded his arms threateningly, while the latter stood slightly bent over with his hands in his pockets. I could not hear their words but I watched them closely. Finally Jean the Nightbird stepped back and I heard him say, "That I won't allow. If he makes a racket we'll tie him up proper."

Guénolé shrugged his shoulders. Then he began making preparations to shift the sails and tack, for the wind had changed direction and was now blowing from the west. Jean the Nightbird approached me and said in a low voice, without looking me in the eye, "Little Morgat, do you know how to swim?"

"Yes."

"Then go to the stern and lie down as if you had given up your idea and were preparing to sleep. Be sure to take off your shoes. When you see Guénolé and myself raising the storm jib, you'll have a chance to slip into the water. Good luck to you! Things have taken a bad turn, but I'm not to blame. Don't ever forget what a favor I'm doing you. After you're gone Guénolé is going to demand an explanation."

With that he went back to the bow. A moment later a fire was lit on the shore and a cannon shot replied to its signal. The coast-guard boat, apprised of our presence, was revealing its position to the pursuers on the shore. At once I slid over the stern and into the water, which was not as cold as I had feared. I struck out, as silently as possible, in the direction of the fire.

There was another detonation, and a cannon ball whizzed over my head. There was a rock in my path and I climbed up on it for a moment's rest. Looking around me I saw the coast-guard boat distinctly. A flurry of smoke detached itself from the prow and a third cannon shot rang in my ears. The coast guards had sighted Guénolé's boat and were giving chase, as he, with all his sails unfurled, fled at full tilt toward the south. Far away

in this direction, I saw another fire, apparently intended to show which way he was going. He and Charlot were skillful navigators, no doubt of that.

After my short rest on the rock I started swimming again, holding the sword between my teeth, which did not exactly facilitate breathing. I was a strong swimmer and after a hundred strokes or so my feet touched bottom. I stood up and started to wade stealthily ashore. Suddenly I heard voices among the overhanging rocks.

"By God," swore a not unfamiliar voice, "that dog will soon be trapped, you'll see!"

And another voice, even more easily recognizable, chimed in, "Here's hoping the boy isn't aboard!"

I stepped onto the beach, raising my arms and dripping water, and shouted. "Mr. Burns! It's me! . . . Little Morgat . . . Yves-Marie . . ."

"God help us!"

"Yes, Kilvinec, it's me . . . it's me, Mr. Burns. . . I'm coming."

Two or three figures climbed down from the rocks and a hand—that of Mr. Burns—was held out to mine.

"Where's my father?"

"You'll see him in a moment. Hold onto my hand, Yves-Marie, and follow me."

Following the path, we came up onto a cliff. Near a fire, some men armed with guns were scanning the sea.

"God be praised, we have him with us!" said Mr. Burns.

The tall, slender figure of my father, followed by a sergeant of the coast guard, detached itself from the group.

"Father!" I called out.

He held out his arms and I sobbed as I embraced him.

66

"There, there, my boy!" he murmured, running his hand through my hair. "What a state you're in!"

I was laughing and crying at the same time. Kilvinec brought me a bowl of cider, heated over the fire.

"Drink this, Little Morgat; it will do you good. You'll tell us all about it later."

The cider was so hot that I could only sip it. But soon I felt my body come to life, my stiffened fingers relax, and the blood course through my veins. Around my father, as he thanked Mr. Burns, were Kilvinec, half a dozen men from the provost-marshal's office, and some coast guards.

"Look," said their sergeant. "Other fires are lighting up to the south. And they're not lit by the wreckers, like the ones we put out yesterday. The whole coast is on the alert and they won't be able to land. Before dawn they'll be taken."

"You don't know that dog of a Guénolé," said Kilvinec. "He could slip through a sieve."

"Is Jean the Nightbird with him?" Mr. Burns asked me.

I nodded assent.

"It was he that kidnapped you, then?" asked my father.

"Yes . . ."

"Don't question him now, Monsieur Morgat," said Mr. Burns. "The poor fellow's exhausted. You can talk to him tomorrow. I'm coming home with you."

And, turning to the coast-guard sergeant, he added, "You don't need me any longer. The man you're looking for is in the boat with Guénolé. Perhaps they're both prisoners already."

My father, Mr. Burns, and I went our way, leaving Kilvinec, whose acquaintance with the ins and outs of the coast made him quite invaluable, behind us. Since my clothes had not had time to be dried out by the fire Kilvinec threw his cloak around me and put his white woolen cap on my head.

A coach, with heavy leather curtains, was waiting on the road half a mile inland. Its dark bulk and the profiles of two sturdy horses stood out against the somber sky that overhung the moors. Before climbing in I feasted my eyes on the spectacle of the third dawn that I had witnessed since I had run away. Suddenly I felt faint and slipped on the running board. Mr. Burns grasped my arm. Soon I was installed on the cushions with a blanket wrapped around my legs; I was smiling all over. I was dimly aware of the way the coach jolted over the bumpy road, but all of a sudden I went off to sleep.

7

My absence from the academy was excused on grounds of illness, and I returned to the study of Cicero and geometry. Needless to say, I did not breathe a word of what I had seen.

When Nicolas came one evening after supper to see me, I gave him back his sword as clean as when he had lent it to me; he asked no embarrassing questions. He spoke of the arrival of a new fencing master, who taught dancing as well and wore the red uniform of the Karrer regiment. I nodded my head, but my thoughts were still on my recent adventure.

Mr. Burns continued to come every night to play chess with my father.

"You can thank this good man for your safe return," my father kept saying. "If it weren't for him you wouldn't be here."

Mr. Burns made a self-effacing gesture and pushed a piece across the chessboard. Upon his advice my father had not been too severe, but evening by evening he extracted from me more details of my escapade. Much as I wanted to keep it to myself, the truth leaked out. I learned, on the other hand, that Mr. Burns had been the first to suspect Jean the Nightbird. This was quite surprising, for he had never seen me in his company. He knew nothing about the traffic in carved figurines, and my father had not even mentioned the convict's name until the day after my disappearance. As a matter of fact my father considered Jean the Nightbird a victim of society rather than a criminal. His daily readings in the philosophy of the Enlightenment and his innate good nature caused him to have an indulgent view of the human race.

I learned, too, how it had come about that Mr. Burns and my father were waiting for me at the shore. It was all perfectly natural, as Mr. Burns explained it. My father had put him on the right track when he finally mentioned Jean the Nightbird's name. Then it came out that I had been seen entering Thomas the Souse's tavern. After this point his explanation was less clear. How did it happen, I wondered, that he had searched the coast just at the point where the wreckers—the accomplices of Guénolé —had lit the misleading fires? Did he have no more than the instincts of an old sea dog to guide him? It had required considerable savvy to stake out a plan in collaboration with the coast guard and the provost-marshal's men. Mr. Burns gave patient and kindly answers to my most searching questions, but I had a feeling that he was saying no more than he wanted to say. When I was too insistent he filled his pipe with tobacco and said, with a wink at my father, "Little Morgat, we sailors have a good sense of smell and certain powers of divination. You weren't so difficult to trace. Like Tom Thumb, you scattered pebbles along the way."

My father scratched his chin and lost himself in thought, while Mr. Burns, with his eyes on the chessboard, went on talking for my benefit.

"There's more adventure on a chessboard than on the seven seas. Aren't you cured of your yearning for independence and the great world?"

"Of course, Mr. Burns. But how did you know that Jean the Nightbird would set sail on Guénolé's boat?"

"I don't know Jean the Nightbird except by his name, which has been on everyone's lips in recent days. Your father tells me that he isn't a bad fellow. I'd like to believe him, although I'm not so sure that there are saints in the penitentiary. Where Jean the Nightbird was concerned I had my reservations. But the chase was conducted by the coast guards and the provost-marshal's men. Your father and I went along simply because of our concern for you."

"No, my friend," my father interrupted. "You led us to the spot. The merit is all yours."

"Occasionally I have a bright idea," said Mr. Burns modestly. "But tell me some more about this Jean the Nightbird, Little Morgat. I wish you had the same gift for portraiture as your friend Nicolas."

"I'm afraid I haven't," I replied. "You're quite right; Nicolas could produce his likeness in a jiffy. All I can tell you is that he's a tall, powerfully built man. He has a long face, a little like . . ."

"Like a carrot," put in Marianne, who was listening at the kitchen door. "He's as ugly as the devil and has the devil's hairy ears. Old Anne used to say that he went around hawking the seven capital sins in the country fairs of Finistère. He has an unholy fear of holy water, I can tell you."

"You don't exactly like him, do you, Marianne?" said Mr. Burns with a laugh.

"That I don't!"

We all joined in the laughter. Mr. Burns, holding his pipe in one hand, slapped his thigh with the other. Just then the front door was pushed open and Nicolas, his portfolio under his arm, burst into the room humming a tune. He swept his hat off his head, put the portfolio down on a chair, and greeted the entire company.

"Sit down, Nicolas," said my father. "You've come in the nick of time; we were just wishing for you. You know Jean the Nightbird, don't you, who used to clean the street in front of our house? Could you make us a sketch of him? Mr. Burns here wants to know what he looks like."

"I don't know how well I remember him, but I'll do my best. . . I'll have a try."

He took a sheet of drawing paper from his portfolio and a pencil from his pocket. Then, after closing his eyes for a moment in reflection, he bent over the table and began to draw. Mr. Burns leaned attentively over his shoulder. Nicolas traced a rough outline, then abruptly tore up the paper, rolled the scraps into a ball, and stuffed them into his pocket.

"No," he said, "I'm going to start all over. Perhaps I shall be more successful." He took a fresh sheet of paper and made the outline again.

"That's him, all right!" I exclaimed.

"The face is his, too, isn't it?" asked Nicolas, holding the sketch at arm's length and examining it.

Mr. Burns took it into his hand and scrutinized it in his turn.

"May I?" he asked, setting it down on the table and, with a pencil of his own, adding a narrow scar between the right ear and the eyebrow. "Isn't that an improvement?"

"You must have known him," I said with amazement. "It's quite true that he has just such a scar."

"Yes, I recognize him. I'll tell you more about him later." And, turning to my father, he added, "Monsieur Morgat, Yves-Marie has been saved from terrible danger. But I still don't understand what impelled the fellow to virtually kidnap him. I fail to see the reason."

We looked in consternation from Mr. Burns to the sketch and from the sketch to Mr. Burns.

Nicolas, who knew practically nothing about my adventure, stared at me in dismay and said in a low voice, "Is that why you wanted to borrow my sword?"

"I'll tell you the whole story tomorrow," I assured him.

"Yes," said Mr. Burns, leaning his head pensively to one side. "I know the man. He's a former seaman whose criminal instincts drove him to becoming a pirate, one of the wiliest and most dangerous fellows you can imagine. By all rights he ought to have been hanged long ago. Jean the Nightbird isn't his real name, of course; he borrowed it from a friend whom he knifed one fine day. Here he was a convict, a ward of the state, but three countries had passed the death sentence upon him. That I can tell you for a fact, because I've read with my own eyes the accusations brought against him at

Savannah, Calicut, and La Guayra. Little Morgat, I shall have no peace of mind until I know for what purpose he tried to trap you."

"I know his purpose," I said impulsively, forgetting that I had promised not to divulge it.

I bit my tongue, but it was too late. My father and Mr. Burns were staring at me.

"Why haven't you told us?" asked my father.

"Because I gave my word that I'd keep his secret."

"At that time you didn't know about the crimes he has committed. The king's justice must be served, and you can consider yourself released from your oath."

"He told me he'd heard about the return of Petit-Radet and wanted to win the reward offered for his capture. Petit-Radet, he said, had stripped him of his honor, and his chief aim in breaking out of the penitentiary was to obtain revenge and rehabilitation."

"I don't know much about Petit-Radet," said Mr. Burns; "nothing more than what's common knowledge. But I have an idea that Jean the Nightbird belonged to his pirate crew. These gentlemen of fortune have a way of falling out, and it wouldn't surprise me if a quarrel between them were behind the present story."

At this point my father repeated the words he had said every evening since my return: "I hope this narrow escape will be a lesson to you!" And, with a sigh, he added: "Of course I should have watched over you more carefully."

The days had grown long, and the feel of summer was in the air. For three months I had put my escapade behind me. The details had slipped from my memory, but the mystery remained unsolved. I was getting on with my studies, and my good marks made it seem likely that in the autumn I should wear the blue uniform with red braid of the artillery school.

Mr. Jerome Burns was tutoring me in English and natural history. He approached this latter subject in the spirit of the great naturalist Buffon, that is, with a sensibility and a feeling for picturesque detail that aroused my enthusiasm. Like his favorite philosopher Helvetius —whose works were, of course, roundly condemned by my masters—Mr. Burns was a man of broad knowledge. His experience of real life and his love of nature lent him a warmth I found sadly lacking in my professors. Other intellectual giants of our time—Lamarck, the chemists Rouelle and Lavoisier, and Diderot—had all enriched his mind. It was of them that he spoke to me, sometimes in the back room of my father's shop and sometimes in his cheerful lodgings at Recouvrance, where the landlady Madame Le Meur served us cups of steaming coffee, whose fragrance filled the whole house.

Mr. Burns hated the abstract reasoning of metaphysics and mathematics and preferred to make his points by experimentation. What inspired my youthful enthusiasm and hence my affection for him was his acquaintance with faraway places and peoples. He described them so vividly that I could see in my mind's eye a series of enchanting landscapes, the flora and fauna that clothe the earth and make it such a thing of wonder. All in all, my new friend exercised a growing influence over me. The high-mindedness of his slightest remarks gave me a warm and happy feeling. And my father, who had used to call me his "wild puppy," appreciated Mr. Burns's calming effect upon my somewhat rebellious nature.

Now that the warm weather was so inviting we went for walks, either in the vicinity of the harbor or in the back country, where the mimosa was in bloom. Mr. Burns often compared the vegetation of our corner of Brittany, which owes its mild climate to warm ocean currents, to that of Florida.

The docks along the Penfeld were my favorite goals. Gesturing with his silver-knobbed cane Mr. Burns discoursed on the different ships at anchor in the harbor or, farther inland, in the shadow of the Castle. War preparations made this area more active than usual, producing a medley of colorful sights and sounds upon which we feasted our eyes and ears.

All the inmates of the penitentiary were hard at work unloading merchandise and arms. Among the piles of boards and pyramids of barrels there were pieces of fighting equipment, cannons and cannon balls waiting to be put aboard the warships lying in the harbor. The town was teeming with soldiers and sailors who, in spite of the nightly curfew, filled the sections of Kéravel and the Seven Saints with commotion. The "Pont Merdou" had become a center of brawling, and the local constabulary had to call on naval police for help. At dusk, bands of sailors in blue-and-white striped bell-bottom trousers and red jackets, with black soft-leather caps on their heads, invaded the town. They moved arm in arm, in long lines, barricading the streets and terrifying cats and women. None of the townspeople wanted to venture out, even with a torch or lantern, after dark. And yet we were accustomed to this kind of disorder and knew that the sailors were more noisy than rough. It was inevitable that, when they came ashore, they should break loose from the harsh discipline to which they were submitted at sea, and their officers were the first to stand up for them when they got in trouble.

Soldiers marched every day down the Rue de Siam, on their way to the camp at Paramé. We saw the regiment of Erlach, in red coats with black collars and facings over a white jacket, the famous Picardy regiment, in uniforms completely white, and the Burgundy regiment, in white coats with gray facings and a crimson collar, which lent a glow to wearers' faces.

The cavalry, on the other hand, rode down the Cours d'Ajot, and the small boys of the town almost broke their necks running when they heard the fifes and drums. Prancing in front of the horses, they escorted the "masters," as the cavalrymen were called, down the street. A regiment of green-and-white dragoons, whose helmets were ornamented with a fur band and a horse tail, preceded by twenty drummers, aroused much enthusiasm. A picturesque caravan of canvas-covered carts followed behind. The Mestre-de-Camp regiment, with dark-blue coats and crimson trimmings, was quartered for two days in the town. A magnificent ball was given in honor of its officers, and all the local nobility attended.

In the company sometimes of Nicolas and sometimes of Mr. Burns, I drank in all these sights, unaware of the horrors of war that lurked behind the dazzling uniforms and thundering regimental bands. Nicolas, too, was overcome with joy. He stuck his elbow into my ribs and shouted, "What a wealth of colors! I'll never have enough talent to put any more than a pale reflection of them on canvas."

On the morning that the Mestre-de-Camp regiment left town there was an incident, apparently unimportant, which led to the renewal of connections with Jean the Nightbird, Petit-Radet, and some other minor but equally dubious characters. It was a hot day, and I was walking

with Mr. Burns on the Esplanade in front of the Castle. We were sitting together on a flat rock when our attention was caught by the elegant maneuvers of a schooner approaching the mouth of the Penfeld. Mr. Burns had taught me to appreciate the subtleties of navigation, and I couldn't resist clapping my hands in admiration of such a perfect example of his precepts. "You're quite right," he said; "the captain knows his trade." And when the sails were furled we both voiced our admiration.

"Since she's anchoring near the Castle," I said, "let's go have a look at her from close by."

We went down a goat path, which led to a narrow terrace near the road circling the Castle.

Only a few swimming strokes away the ship was gliding to rest. A rope squeaked against first the capstan and then the hawsehole, and the anchor slipped into the water.

"Damn it! . . . I mean, by George!" Mr. Burns exclaimed, "if that isn't . . ." He stopped short, blushed, and beat his hand against his forehead. "If I let myself swear like that," he said to me, "it's because for a second I thought I was seeing a ghost. Can you, with your good eyes, read the name?"

His eyes were keen enough, but in order to comply with his request I scrutinized the name inscribed under the poop. *"Rose of Savannah,"* I told him.

"That just goes to show you, Little Morgat, that a man mustn't eat too heavy a breakfast or believe in the figments of his imagination. The ship she reminds me of— long since at the bottom of the Sargasso Sea—was called the *Mercy*."

"The *Mercy?*"

"Yes, and I was in command," said Mr. Burns with a sigh.

8

The next day, as soon as I had left the academy, I felt a strong urge to look more closely at the schooner, and climbed up on a rock in front of the Tour de la Madeleine, whence I had an excellent view. The *Rose of Savannah* was, indeed, a fine ship, built on racing lines. The hull was blue and the porthole lids red, while the bulwarks were outlined by a narrow strip of gold. But its greatest glory was the old-fashioned figurehead at the bow: a black girl with a rose between her breasts and a provocative smile. I paid as yet little attention to women's charms, but it seemed to me that her exotic lips might well pronounce the magic words opening the door to adventure, and I was ready to follow her bidding. Later on Mr. Burns told me that I was very naïve.

There was only one man on deck, a tall fellow with graying hair and a pock-marked face. He was sitting on a coil of rope, one end of which he was splicing. He whistled as he worked and did not so much as look in my direction. After I had come down from the rock and just before I reached the Seven Saints district, I saw a group of convicts engaged in stacking grenades and cannon balls in front of a cargo-carrying corvette. Their guard stood some distance away, chatting with an uncommonly stout, red-haired woman.

I was reminded of Jean the Nightbird and very nearly spoke to one of the convicts who had often worked alongside him. But I had promised my father to have no more to do with any inmate of the penitentiary, and so I held back the words that were on the tip of my tongue, thereby missing a most unusual chance to get an inside story of the flight of Jean the Nightbird and Raspberry.

I arrived home just as Mr. Jerome Burns was pushing open the shop door.

"Hello there, Yves-Marie! I take it the *Rose of Savannah* hasn't yet weighed anchor. That's a very fine figurehead, isn't it?"

As usual, Mr. Burns was a mind reader. He leaned against the polished oak counter and enquired about the health of my father, who showed obvious delight in his visit. Then he asked to see a collection of cutlasses, of the kind that sailors carry in a leather sheath on their belts. He bought the handsomest among them and slipped it contentedly into an inside pocket of his dark-blue jacket. Then he sat, as was his habit, on the counter, with one foot on the floor and the other dangling and offered a pinch of snuff to my father, who took it in order not to offend him. Soon he began talking of his despotic mistress, the sea, and of the dead cities of India, inhabited by insolent baboons, chattering parrots, and timorous tropical birds. For our benefit he gave an imitation of the fearful sound which Drake claimed to have heard at Cape Horn. He spoke in a grave, gentle voice, and I listened with my mouth hanging open, so persuasive were his words.

"At Caracas or, more exactly, off La Guayra, I had my first sight of the black pirate flag flying over a two-master with sixteen bronze cannons that gleamed in the sun. Our skipper, Joris Truda de Walcheren, made the sign of the cross, but the pirate, to our surprise, took no notice of us. A few minutes later he hauled down the black flag and ran up a yellow one, showing that the plague was raging aboard. Then he sailed southward, disappearing behind the horizon, as if he had no other place to go."

"Haven't you ever fought with pirates, Mr. Burns?"

"If I said yes, just to give you pleasure, I'd be telling you a lie."

One of the places Mr. Burns most liked to talk about was the Antilles, which he described as baskets of fruit and flowers floating on the water. He knew the Latin names of plants and their medical and industrial uses, and spoke with admiration of the natives' understanding of the virtues of various herbs, particularly those that produce longevity. He did not believe in the famous "Flying Dutchman," of which Kilvinec had so often told us, but he did think that the sea serpent existed, as the remnant of a species wiped out by the biblical Flood.

Now, happy in the purchase of the cutlass, Mr. Burns bade us farewell. My father urged him to share our dinner, but he refused.

82

"You do well to listen to this man, Yves-Marie," said my father after he had gone away. "What he knows, he knows at firsthand and has seen with his own eyes. That's what gives weight to his opinions. When you're older you'll appreciate him even more. You're a bit dreamy and impulsive, you know. Not that I'd have you different from what you are. Sometimes dreaminess is a way, as good as any other, of thinking before you speak."

I was always happy when my father spoke to me in a confidential tone or when he discoursed, in highly poetical fashion, of the objects in his shop. Of every one of them he had a story to tell, and one which illustrated his taste and discrimination.

After we had finished our meal the purser of the *Clarisse* came by to order considerable quantities of biscuits, tinned beef, and rum. A glass of rum celebrated the transaction and, most exceptionally, I was called in.

"Do you know why I like rum?" my father was saying as he raised his pewter goblet to the level of his eyes. "The fragrance of it reminds me of the garden of Monsieur Lacaussade, the man from Bordeaux who owns so many well-fed slaves and has a face like that of the Emperor Caligula."

To me the fragrance of the rum had less enchantment than the figurehead at the bow of the *Rose of Savannah*. Somehow I associated the black girl with Mr. Burns; both of them held for me the same sort of inexplicable fascination.

The purser of the *Clarisse* was a stout, red-faced man whose powerful thighs and broad shoulders almost burst the seams of his red trousers and iron-gray coat with red trimmings. He sniffed the rum appreciatively and winked a knowing eye.

"By Bacchus and the ladies, with all due respect! This is something to warm the innards! I propose a toast to Petit-Radet and his swift ascent to the gallows!"

"Petit-Radet?" said my father with surprise.

"What, Monsieur Morgat? You didn't know? It's in preparation for the pursuit of that slippery eel that the *Clarisse* is taking on stores. It even seems that the *Néère,* a frigate with forty cannons and a crew of three hundred men, will be joining our humble civilian forces. Our job is merely to serve as a decoy, but we shall have our share of glory. There's a surprise in store for him!"

Just then we saw walking down the Rue de Siam a dozen officers of the Royal Navy, in their blue, gold-braided coats, red trousers, and red stockings. They were conversing in whispers but with considerable animation. At their head were Count de Guichen, the lieutenant-general in command of the local naval forces, and Count Le Begue, who had the rank of captain and the post of artillery director.

"Didn't I tell you?" said the purser. "There you have the top brass of the *Néère* before your eyes!"

Some soldiers of the regiment of Brest followed after. We knew well their blue coats with scarlet facings, their white breeches and the white gaiters that came up above their knees. After all, this was the regiment of our town and we cherished it as we did everything connected with local history. Monsieur de Kerrion, the commanding officer, came from near by and enjoyed the highest esteem. As for the regiment, it was even more popular than the Swiss Karrer regiment, formerly in the service of that India Company which had gone out of existence some years before.

"You're quite right," said my father. "The regiment of

Brest seems to be sending out a company of fusiliers in battle dress. There must be a reason for these goings on; perhaps something quite out of the ordinary is going to happen."

For my part, although I did not enter into the conversation, I listened attentively. The words of the purser played upon my imagination and I felt sure that great events were at hand. "There's no smoke without fire," Pillawer had said. "If there's so much talk about Petit-Radet then a devil who's his spitting image must have cast anchor near by."

My first thought was to tell Mr. Burns that the rumor of Petit-Radet's presence was acquiring new credibility. Were not soldiers leaving their barracks, and ships taking on stores to track him down?

In front of the "Firebrand" Nicolas was flirting with Manon. He suspended this pleasant occupation just long enough to listen to my story and to cast doubt on my suppositions. "Premature," he called them. I did not linger. The ferryman rowed me across the river, and I made my way through the narrow, terraced streets to the house of Madame Le Meur, surrounded now by blooming lilac bushes. I knocked once, twice, at the door, until I heard footsteps in the hall and the plaintive voice of the landlady: "Who's there?"

"Yves-Marie Morgat, Madame. I've come to see Mr. Burns."

The door opened, and Madame Le Meur appeared on the threshold. "My good boy, Mr. Burns isn't here. He left a little less than an hour ago."

"He must have gone for a walk," I said disappointedly. "I can come back later or perhaps even wait for him, if you don't mind."

"He went away on horseback, on a stout beast that looked capable of taking him a long way. Besides, he gave me the key to his room and said he might be gone as long as a week."

I scratched my head and said goodbye. With a feeling of bewilderment I went back—this time by the bridge—to Brest.

The day had another surprise in store. Just as I was about to leave the docks and start up the Rue de Siam a peasant in reddish-brown garb barred my way. From under his checkered wool belt he pulled out a folded sheet of paper. Hardly had I taken it into my hand than he disappeared amid a group of onion merchants who had spread out their wares at the corner. Immediately I opened up the paper and, with pounding heart, read the following words: *"Keep your eyes peeled. The villain is not far away and we are close to getting what we are after. Don't let anyone discourage you. When you hear mention of Petit-Radet, write it down and leave the note under the usual stone. Have no fear; we shall soon be rewarded for all our troubles."*

For some days I had not even thought of the obvious author of this anonymous letter. When we are young the past fades quickly. Since returning to my customary comforts and occupations I had forgotten all but the most romantic aspects of my escapade. I had acquired a certain prestige among my school friends, and even the carefree Nicolas had been impressed by what I told him of my story.

I reached home in a troubled frame of mind, which I resolved to conceal from my father. I felt quite sure of my own will power. Hadn't I withstood the temptation of talking to Jean the Nightbird's fellow-convicts only the day before, when the arrival of the *Rose of Savannah* had furnished me with such a pleasant distraction? Yes, I would reread the letter, burn it, and think about it no more.

When I walked into the shop my father was busy with his accounting. I told him at once that Mr. Burns had gone off to an unknown destination, riding a horse which I described as a "splendid charger."

"That's surprising," said my father. "He said nothing to me about it. Something very urgent must have come up all of a sudden to cause him to leave without notice."

And he plunged back into his account book. Since supper wasn't yet ready I went up to my room and reread the mysterious letter. My eyes strayed to the shelves, where among my books I had set up Jean the Nightbird's carved and painted figures. I took down a captain of the Royal Navy who might have been a portrait—even if verging on caricature—of Monsieur de Bois-Baudru, commander of the *Néère;* he was a long-legged man whose noble bearing inspired respect and fear. The uniform was an exact replica, from head to foot, of the one he wore, from the gold-braided tricorn hat to the silver buckles on the shoes. The blue coat had gold trimmings and so did the red jacket and breeches. Monsieur de Bois-Baudru wore white stockings ashore and red ones on shipboard.

As I examined these details I wondered what had become of my convict friend. His letter gave proof that he had not been arrested. But where had he taken refuge? And what about the red-nosed Raspberry and the nefarious Thomas the Souse? Where were these "companions of the night" as he called them? This mystery, which had burst in upon my well-ordered life, would give me no peace. With my necktie unknotted and my hair pushed back untidily from my forehead, I paced up and down the room.

"I won't answer," I said to myself. "I don't want to do anything that would displease Mr. Burns or my father." And in order to fend off the temptation I tore the paper into shreds, threw them out the window, and watched them flutter away over the roof. But I did not recover my peace of mind. I was haunted by the unknown figure of Petit-Radet, whom I imagined in the most bizarre guises. Impulsively I wrote a note in answer to Jean the Nightbird's, promising myself that I would destroy it in the same fashion.

After supper I stepped out for a breath of air. There was still a hum of activity and a feeling of war. Here and there a ship's lantern was reflected on the water as the vessel moved stealthily out to sea. Along the docks of the Penfeld a hundred flickering lights lit up the embarkation of troops going to the camp at Paramé. Every now and then I heard the ruffle of a drum, the blast of a horn, a plaintive air played by a fife or an oboe. Turning my back on this shadow-show I moved like an automaton in the direction of Kéravel. At the corner of an alley near "Neptune's Wood," which was now closed down, I saw the stone that marked the beginning of all my troubles. There was a thin coating of moss upon it. I lifted it up and slipped under it the answer to Jean the Nightbird's letter; I had not torn it up after all.

When I got home—which did not take me long—I found my father at the door, talking with Monsieur de Pinville and Monsieur de Forster, a lieutenant of the Karrer regiment. My father closed the shutters of the shop and went with his friends to the "Firebrand." As for me, after bantering for a few minutes with Marianne, I went up to my room. But it was quite impossible to sleep. I blew out my candle and went to look down from the window at the Rue de Siam and the portion of the docks extending as far as the Castle. It was a beautiful night. The sea breeze had brought relief from the heat generated by old walls which had roasted all day in the sun.

But my temples were throbbing and I was too perturbed by my recent action to enjoy the scene. What an idiot I was to have answered the letter! To have linked my fortune, again, with that of Jean the Nightbird was sure to lead to all sorts of complications. And for the first time my vision of adventure was tinged with human blood. At the end of the path onto which I had let Jean the Nightbird impel me I could see murder. All of a sudden I was so terrified that I resolved to go take my note away from under the stone.

The absence of my father made it easy for me to go. Without bothering to put on my hat I tiptoed down the stairs, taking care not to awaken Marianne, and slipped out the back door into an alley. Once outside I broke into a run, hugging the walls all the way to the stone. But when I lifted it up I saw at once that the note was no longer there. For a moment I did not know what to do. Then, shaking with fear, I ran as fast as I could back to the house, where I collapsed on my bed, my face covered with perspiration. I could not close an eye for thinking about what I had written. And yet there was nothing very compromising about it: *"The* Néère *is boarding men and supplies in order to track down the man you are looking for. It looks like a big operation. That's all I can tell you."*

Finally, however, sleep did overcome me.

9

Actually the flight of Jean the Nightbird and the guard who was his accomplice had had very few repercussions. Such occurrences were not rare at the penitentiary. And the consequences were these: a cannon shot dispersed the sea gulls from the Penfeld, and the coast guards scoured the countryside until, whether or not they caught the fugitive, the whole episode was forgotten. The townspeople went their way, except, perhaps, for a few youngsters whose imaginations had been ignited. As for the penitentiary officials, they summed it up with an aphorism: "One failure to ten successes."

I didn't see it the same way, but then I was personally involved. In spite of the sound advice of my father and

Mr. Burns I was still tempted by adventure. No one spoke any more of my escapade and I remembered its romantic side rather than its danger.

How sorry I was, never to have seen Jean the Nightbird's statuette inspired by the memory of Petit-Radet! When I mingled with the Sunday crowd on the Esplanade or with the buyers and sellers at the weekly market set up on the Rue de Siam I was always picking out a face and saying to myself: "Couldn't that be Petit-Radet?" There was plenty of choice, because Brest abounded in leather-faced sea dogs. Who was to say whether they were honest men like Joachim Goas, the merchant-ship captain, or gentlemen of fortune who sailed under the black flag with skull and crossbones?

I was sure that my instinct would guide me, but more than once it played me false. For days I mistakenly identified Petit-Radet in the person of a sail maker serving aboard the *Flore,* a frigate of the Royal Navy in the process of being equipped for war.

It was the end of July and the academy had closed its doors for the summer. I had won admission to the artillery school of Metz and my father wanted me to be free to enjoy myself until October. A good part of my thoughts were occupied by my future career, but Petit-Radet was always at the back of my mind. Was he lurking off the coast or in some village of lower Brittany? Or was it true, as some people said, that he had taken to the hills, along with a woman bandit who specialized in holding up innocent travelers?

"Devil take the two of them!" I said to myself as I walked toward the Castle. Nicolas had set up his easel in its shadow and was making money by sketching portraits of the soldiers and sailors who strolled by. Several

91

officers of the Brest regiment had ordered a portrait, and Monsieur de Forster had commissioned him to paint one of his daughter Isabelle, who had recently become engaged to a young navy lieutenant.

Just now Nicolas was surrounded by half a dozen soldiers in fatigue uniform, with bandanas around their heads. Some of their companions straddled benches, in tandem formation, each one of them combing the hair of the fellow in front of him. I sat down for a few minutes beside Nicolas and watched him at work. Then, feeling slightly bored, I got up and walked in the direction of the path which led to the road circling the Castle. My heart pounded when I saw before me the *Rose of Savannah,* riding motionlessly and with all sails neatly furled, under the guardianship, as it were, of the shapely black divinity at the prow. I lingered for some time, my thoughts wandering far beyond my native horizons, beyond any reasonable perspective of my future. As dusk fell and all over the harbor ship lanterns began to light up, I suddenly remembered that my father had given me an errand to do. I was to take a watch he had repaired to Captain Joachim Goas, whose ship, the *Marie-Cardez,* lay anchored not far from the *Rose of Savannah.* Captain Goas was a reputable and skilled navigator, the father of five children, one of whom went to school with me and intended to enter the priesthood.

In a few seconds I was down on the docks. The ships, with their sails rolled around the yards, looked like an assembly of ghosts. I ran by the *Rose of Savannah* and, a few moorings farther on, came to the *Marie-Cardez.* A lantern was bobbing up and down in the vicinity of the bow, but in the darkness I could not make out the identity of the bearer.

"Ho there, aboard the *Marie-Cardez!*" I shouted.

"Ho!"

"Send me a boat! Is that you, Monsieur Goas? I'm Yves-Marie Morgat, and I'm bringing you back a watch from my father."

"Wait a minute, boy. I'm coming."

The lantern moved out of sight and a few minutes later I heard oars squeaking in the oarlocks of a small boat. Captain Goas took the watch and told me to thank my father.

"We're leaving at dawn. If you want to see a fine sailing, with a favorable wind at the stern, get up early and watch us from the heights of Lanninon."

"I'm afraid that's too early for me," I answered, laughing.

"Devil of a Little Morgat!"

He went back to his brig while I waited for a few minutes, listening to the squeaking oars and watching the lantern throw its light on the water. The dock was silent, and a dim lamp lit the steep goat path that led past the Tour de la Madeleine up to the Castle. The path was littered with small, pointed stones, and was foul-smelling. I don't really know why I chose to take it. Halfway up I stopped to rest. Standing on a rock with another sheltering rock above, I looked straight down at the deck of the *Rose of Savannah,* lit up by a lantern which stood on a barrel with a tarpaulin thrown across it.

In a ray of yellow light I made out a pock-marked face. The owner was talking with someone else who was hidden by the darkness. Instinctively I crouched on my heels in order not to be seen. I listened attentively but above the pounding of my own heart I could hear no more than whispered, fragmentary phrases. At a certain point I heard the pock-marked man say, "We must give orders to go away one by one. . ." Just at this moment the shrill blast of a whistle caused me to start. Apparently it was even more startling to the two men aboard the *Rose of Savannah*. The pock-marked one picked up the lantern and went over to the railing, while scurrying footsteps made it seem that his companion was running away. There was a loud thud of something falling on the deck. Leaning against the railing with one hand on a ratline, the pock-marked man hummed to himself and looked down at the deserted dock. After a few minutes of silence I heard two very low whistles. The pock-marked man turned back toward the deck and said, "False alarm!"

The other man reappeared, whispered a few words into his ear and leaned over the railing, in his turn, to scrutinize the dock. His face was hidden from me by the upraised hood of his sailor's coat. Now, having judged that the coast was clear, he walked out on the plank that connected the ship with the shore. With a few quick steps he disappeared among the shadows of the rocks at the foot of the Castle.

The rapid succession of these events left me perplexed. Just as I was pulling myself together I heard footsteps on the path. The figure of a man—heavy-set yet light-footed—almost brushed me as it went by. The mysterious individual stumbled on a stone and swore in Breton dialect. I recognized the voice—or fancied I recognized it—as that of Mr. Jerome Burns. No, this was quite impossible! Before I could recover my self-possession he was far away and I had not the presence of mind to pursue him. A mixture of astonishment, fear, and curiosity had left me limp. With hanging head I stumbled home,

95

almost falling and breaking my neck on the stones along the way.

"You took a long time," said my father. "I was beginning to be worried."

"He's a headstrong boy," said Marianne. "He'll finish on the gallows one day."

I made no reply. My overactive imagination was filled with the memory of the pock-marked man and his companion, and I shut my eyes in order to make them stand out more vividly in my mind. I remembered the conversation between Mr. Burns and myself on the day when we had watched the arrival of the *Rose of Savannah* together. As we admired the dexterity of its skipper I had asked him if he knew anyone aboard. And he had answered, "You don't suppose I know every sailor in the world, do you, Little Morgat?" Obviously he was not the man who had been conversing with the pock-marked member of the mysterious schooner's crew.

"Get yourself to bed," said my father. "You're half-asleep already."

I lost no time in obeying, for I was anxious to be alone in my own room. The night was hot, and I threw open the window and blew out the candle. The clear, starry night bore no trace of evil, and the street below was deserted except for the cat from the "Firebrand", which was scratching among the garbage.

I closed the window and got undressed in the dark. Before going to bed I said a prayer, asking vaguely for God's blessing on my father and on my new mentor and friend. But who, exactly, was Mr. Burns? The respectable pensioner who had lodgings in Recouvrance or the mysterious man who had so hastily left the *Rose of Savannah*.

The next morning I was awakened by the smell of a thick soup and pancakes made of good black wheat. I ran my hand over my face in order to sweep my doubts away.

From the back room of the shop I heard the bell ring and then the rap of a cane against the counter with which Mr. Burns always made known his presence. His arrival was like a burst of sunshine between two clouds and I rushed forward to grasp his hands.

"Good fellow, Little Morgat!" he said with a kindly laugh. At once I felt reassured.

"We're happy to have you back," said my father. "We've spoken of you often, and missed you."

"I've been in Quimper, on some business connected with an inheritance. And what's become of the *Rose of Savannah?*" he added, turning in my direction.

"She's still anchored in front of the Castle," I said, involuntarily blushing.

Actually, Mr. Burns's return dispelled all my suspicions and indeed made me almost ashamed of them. However, the *Rose of Savannah* had set fire to my easily inflamed imagination. I was of an age to give human form and substance to my desires, and the ebony girl at the prow of the idling ship seemed to incarnate them. Meanwhile, the day after Mr. Burns's return I decided to speak to my father about an idea that had been tormenting me for some weeks. He was alone in the shop and the moment seemed propitious.

"Father, I'd like to ask you a favor."

"What is it, Yves-Marie?"

"You promised me a reward for having passed my artillery-school examinations. I'd like you to change the sign on our shop and to give it a new name, one I would know would please Mr. Burns. It's partly on account of his tutoring that I got such good marks."

"And what is the new name that would be so pleasing to him?"

" 'The Anchor of Mercy,' instead of 'The Coral Anchor.' And I could get Nicolas to design the sign."

"I don't see how I can say no. But what would Mr. Burns like so much about the word 'mercy'?"

"That was the name of his ship. And when he spoke of her to me I realized how very attached to her he was."

"Very good," my father said, smiling; "and may the name be of good omen! The anchor of mercy is the last hope of salvation."

I jumped with joy, thanked my father, and rushed out to look for Nicolas at the "Firebrand." I wanted to strike while the iron was hot.

"Hurrah for the Royal Artillery!" Nicolas exclaimed when I came in. He was sitting in front of a carafe of wine with his pipe in one hand while with the other he chucked the chin of Manon. I sat down beside him and, after a scolding from the proprietor, Manon brought me a drink.

"Nicolas, you must outdo yourself!" I said without preamble. "I've come to ask you something, and if you say yes you'll make me very happy."

"By Bacchus and his maidservant, Manon, I swear to make you a happy man! What is it you want?"

As I set forth my idea Nicolas took out his drawing pad and started to sketch. "We'll put the anchor in the center with a blazing sun above it . . . And in the background a schooner, like the one anchored in front of the

Castle, and a streamer with the words 'The Anchor of Mercy' . . ."

"Perfect, Nicolas! A thousand thanks. And I want to have it in a hurry. Mr. Burns is coming to lunch with us the day after tomorrow and I'd like to have my surprise there to greet him."

"I'll paint the sign tomorrow morning, and it will be dry by the end of the day. You can hang it in plenty of time. Now drink your wine and tell me what you've heard about the war. The town is full of bombardiers. Too bad you artillerymen don't wear a bearskin cap like theirs; it would be most becoming."

I was in a mood for joking and clapped him gaily on the shoulder. "How are things going with Manon?" I countered.

"Miserable girl, she's smitten with a sergeant! His mustache must be bigger than his brain, because he's promised to marry her."

The next day Nicolas faithfully went to work and painted what to me seemed a work of art. He did the lettering with his own hand, and this took more time than all the rest. The following morning the sign was hoisted into place, arousing much curiosity among the passers-by. My father was bombarded with questions and finally went inside and barred the door. At the sound of the noon cannon I began to watch out for Mr. Burns, in order to enjoy his surprise. I ran to meet him, my eyes sparkling with excitement, when I saw him turn the corner.

"How happy you look, Little Morgat!" he said by way of greeting.

When we reached the door I told him to look up. At

once he saw the sign and read aloud the words "The Anchor of Mercy." After a moment of silence he shook his head and said with a gentle smile, "You really mustn't call it 'Mercy.' "

I was speechless.

"The name is dear to me, Little Morgat, it's quite true. But that's no reason for such a sign of affection on the part of yourself and your father."

"But we want it that way. My father feels just as happy about it as I do."

"I'll accept, then, Little Morgat, on condition that you promise me to pursue your chosen career and not to dream about running off to sea."

"I'll think about it," I said gaily. "A man sentenced to death always has seven minutes in which to pray."

Mr. Burns wagged his forefinger. "A rascal, that's what you are, Little Morgat! Very well, then; you shall have your seven minutes."

We went inside, where my father shook both of Mr. Burns's hands and Marianne brought in a platter of steaming spiced sausages. All during lunch Mr. Burns held my father spellbound with his conversation. On this particular occasion he set forth social ideas so advanced that they might have come out of the clandestine Paris papers. Every now and then my father raised his hand and said, "I'm sorry, but I can't go that far with you."

But in the end they agreed, since both of them believed in common honesty and respect for the law.

"Look at this boy," said Mr. Burns, changing the subject. "He's dreaming of pirates and sea battles and boarding parties . . ."

I thought to myself: "At last the question's up for discussion."

"I know," said my father. "When I was his age I hankered after the sea. But here I am, a landlubber."

There was a melancholy smile on his face as he filled his clay pipe with tobacco from a blue-and-white delft jar. Mr. Burns followed his example and then started to talk again, even more animatedly than before.

"When I was a boy the sea was always at the back of my mind. Between the lines of my *De viris illustribus urbis Romae* I read the words: 'You'll find adventure at sea.' Adventure! I've pursued adventure all over the globe, but it's never measured up to my ideal; indeed, I don't think my ideal exists; it's unattainable. A man spends the better part of his life trying to embrace a ghost. Then, with old age, he finds himself fading away without the only real joy, that of a home and family . . ."

"You haven't told us the whole story," I said, looking him in the eye.

"Little Morgat, you can't understand all the tricks of the imagination. If you wait to learn from experience the truth of what I'm telling you, it will be too late."

"The boy is headstrong and stubborn as a mule," said my father. "But at bottom he's a good fellow, and I have the same confidence in him that I have in your ideas. Believe me, my friend, he'll do honor to his blue uniform and his sword."

"I'm sure of that," said Mr. Burns, with a half-kindly, half-malicious smile. After lunch the two men sat down to a game of chess that lasted until evening.

"Guess what time it is!" Mr. Burns exclaimed suddenly, pulling out his watch.

"Time for supper! And you must stay with us in order to make it a perfect day."

"I don't want to take advantage of your hospitality.

And Madame Le Meur may wonder where I am."

"Your excuses don't hold water," my father told him. "And from something I heard this morning, Marianne has a surprise in store—some freshly baked tarts with whipped cream. Don't they tempt you?"

Mr. Burns needed considerable persuading, but at last he gave in.

"There's time for a revenge game before supper is on the table," said my father, setting up the pieces on the chessboard.

10

The week after we had renamed our shop was eventful and somewhat disquieting. Captain Goas came back from a voyage to The Hague, bringing more rumors of war. Pillawer, the peddler, brought gossip from all the market-places between Quimper and Châteaulin. Digwener and Kilvinec had tidbits of news of Petit-Radet.

The entire coast, it seemed, was in fear and trembling at the very mention of his name. Fishing boats did not dare put out to sea and even cutters were temporarily dismissing their crews. At night, in the cafés, there were whispered conversations about the pirate's exploits, and the whistling wind seemed to bear the dying cries of his victims. My father belittled his visitors' stories.

"Come now, don't exaggerate!" he said to Pillawer. "Has anyone seen with his own eyes a victim of Petit-Radet?"

"Petit-Radet is dead," I put in. "Mr. Burns told us that a week ago."

"Dead or not dead," said Pillawer from the other side of the counter, "he's *here*. We feel it in our bones and it prevents us from getting on with the day's work. Young girls won't take their coifs and embroidered aprons out of the drawers to dress up and go out. Peasants are fretting and pining away as if they were office workers. At Merrien, where I was last week, I didn't sell so much as a handkerchief, and after dark no one would stick his head out of the door. Even the blind beggars who play the bagpipes in the marketplaces are silent."

"You're quite right," said Kilvinec, coming in the door. "I've just arrived from Ouessant by way of Le Conquet. The fishing boats are all beached. I ran into Digwener on the docks, and he'll tell you the same thing. He'll be along any minute to buy some rope and biscuits and rum. Between Molène and Quéménez he glimpsed a snow-white brig, which he fancied for a minute was the legendary ghost ship of Jean-Espère-en-Dieu. He crossed himself, and then he saw that the cannons were of the latest model and the sailors standing on the poop deck were not disembodied spirits but men of flesh and blood, and well-fed ones at that."

"That doesn't prove anything," said my father. "Here's Digwener in person. Yves-Marie, give me the coil of rope just above you, so that we shan't keep him waiting."

But Digwener was in no hurry. He was as full of talk as a Spanish galley of doubloons.

"Good day to all!" he said as he came in. "May God

104

protect you! I see you're getting my order ready, Monsieur Morgat. Kilvinec must have spoken for me. Hello there, Kilvinec! This is the second time we meet, and they say that when there are two, a third will follow. . . I'll have some tobacco, too, Monsieur Morgat. It's not for myself but for the coast-guard sergeant of Le Conquet."

"Puerto Rico tobacco?"

"Whatever would satisfy a connoisseur."

"What have you heard since I last saw you?" asked Pillawer, who had sat down on his basket.

"Nothing new. The fellow's at loose on the moors. Some say he's hiding out at Quimperlé. Yesterday a hawker from Vannes was held up on the highway, probably by the gang of that witch they say is living with him. She's dressed one day like a princess and the next like a barmaid. And she's the one that keeps him informed. She even told him about the *Néère,* and he sent a warning to his men. They say his ship's papers are signed by the king of England. Some of the fishermen speak of arming a schooner. But what can six guns do against thirty-seven? Yes, my friends, he has thirty-seven cannons and as many grenades as there are apples in Mahieux's orchard. And do you know how his paramour from the mountains gets her information? Pillawer here has had dealings with the bandits, and he can tell you . . ."

"Bandit yourself!" Pillawer retorted. "What do you mean I've had 'dealings'?"

"Calm down, there," said my father, feeling a fight in the making. "Pillawer's a good fellow, like yourself, Digwener. I want you to taste the liqueur I've just got in from Nantes. If we leave the bandits in peace they won't disturb us. Isn't that so, Kilvinec?"

"I'm not speaking ill of anybody. But I prefer good salt water to mountain air, if you ask me. It's a lot healthier."

The two men's tempers fell as rapidly as they had risen, and they joined in a toast to my father. When they had gone away he said, "No use trying to make head or tail out of all that gossip. Here we are, only a few miles from the coast, and they might be telling us stories of China. I believe Petit-Radet's dead, as Mr. Burns told us. Only ghosts can create so much trouble among the living. And the voice of Merlin the magician is still heard among us."

Just then the doorbell rang and a stranger came into the shop. He wore a brown suit, and bore himself like an old sea hand dressed up in his Sunday best. I noticed immediately one significant thing about him: his pockmarked face. Without saying a word he laid his hat down on the counter and scrutinized the shelves.

"What will you have, sir?" my father asked.

"A ship's lantern; one of the best quality."

"I have just what you want in my stores. Wait just a minute and I'll bring it to you."

Our stores were kept in a big shed in the courtyard back of the house. I was left alone with the stranger and observed him attentively. I could not have sworn that there was any resemblance between him and the pockmarked man I had glimpsed in the dark aboard the *Rose of Savannah*. In fact, I was just thinking that pock-marks were far from uncommon when he said something that made me shudder.

"You are Little Morgat?"

When I nodded, he went on, in a low voice, with his eye on the back door. "I've a message from Jean the Nightbird. He's coming this evening to the stone, you

106

know the one I mean. He says that it is important for you to meet him. And he's bringing with him a little wooden figure of the man he's after. You know whom I mean, don't you?"

As my father appeared at the door, he brusquely changed the subject and asked me if I intended to carry on the business. My father showed him the lantern and, after examining it as carefully as if it were a precious antique, he signified that he would take it with him. At the threshold, while my father's back was turned, he looked at me and held a finger to his lips. The familiar gesture awakened the demon of adventure in my heart.

For the third time Jean the Nightbird was bidding me join my fate to his. The promise of the statuette appealed irresistibly to my curiosity. I remembered the chilly room at "Neptune's Wood," with its smell of stale wine and cider, where the alarm given by Ninon Glao had prevented him from showing me the carved portrait of Petit-Radet. To know what the villain looked like was even more exciting and important now than then. I had no need to stop and think; my mind was made up already. I concentrated my attention on the means of effecting this new excursion into the sordid alleys of Kéravel. The rough men and blatantly provocative women of the underworld were more attractive to me than ever.

There was no question of my walking out the front door after supper. Once more I must bide my time, then crawl out the window and over the rooftop and slide down the rain pipe onto the street below. But this presented no difficulty. Within a few hours I should be in on a secret that was well worth the trouble. For a weapon, this time I took from the drawer under the counter a sailor's cutlass with an English blade and an ivory handle, in a soft leather case. With this attached, out of sight, to the belt of my trousers I felt equipped for any emergency.

While waiting for nightfall I went for a walk in the direction of the Castle, in order to take a surreptitious look at the *Rose of Savannah,* whose prolonged and immobile presence was inexplicably disquieting. Was Jean the Nightbird's messenger the pock-marked man I had glimpsed aboard the mysterious schooner? She might be a pirate ship in disguise, and in any case it seemed likely that she had some connection with the convict's scheme of revenge. Jean the Nightbird had sailed with the notorious John Gow; that he had told me. Yes, everything pointed to the conclusion that he and the *Rose of Savannah* were linked together. And I need not be ashamed of seconding his scheme. Anything that worked against Petit-Radet was for the good of the terrified population.

As I tried to string these hypotheses together I arrived at the dock, in full sight of the fascinating black girl under the bowsprit. The ship's deck was deserted. Under some new tarpaulins there were probably coils of rope, bales of merchandise or, as my romantic imagination would have it, short cannons, which would be revealed only in the presence of the enemy. There was somebody aboard, for from a porthole I heard the strains of, "My Lover Was a Guardsman," a song by Vadé, which was very popular among the military.

The voice trailed off, and a man appeared on the deck. Was he the singer? In any case he was not the pockmarked individual whose identity weighed so heavily on my mind. He went over to the railing and looked down at some children who were playing hopscotch on the dock, then, shoving his hands into his pockets, gave me the benefit of a long stare.

I pretended to be a casual passer-by, captivated by the ship's truly elegant lines. I examined the figurehead, then walked back toward the stern, nodding my head like a connoisseur. During all this time the sailor kept staring at me. As I approached the gangplank he opened a door just under the poop deck, which must have given onto a passageway leading to the powder magazine and the officers' quarters.

"Look," he said simply.

The door was still open, and I felt sure that other unseen eyes were observing me. My interlocutor disappeared for a moment and I heard the murmur of voices. I was just leaning forward, as inconspicuously as possible, in an attempt to catch the words, when he came back up on deck. The sun was still hot and the smell of tar mingled with that of stagnant water.

"Hello there, young gentleman, hello there, sailor!" he called out. "Give me the money for a glass of rum and I'll show you over the fastest merchant ship on the seven seas. It's not often that an apprentice seaman, such as I take you to be, has such an opportunity.

"I'd be glad to stake you to the rum," I answered, "but I don't see how I can come aboard your ship without the skipper's permission."

"Don't worry about that. The captain's not aboard, but the lieutenant is exercising his command, and he'll be delighted to welcome a future officer, one who is obviously dying to accept my invitation."

I stepped onto the gangplank, and a moment later I was standing on the deck of the *Rose of Savannah*. My emotion was so great that I had to catch hold of a shroud, whose rough hemp scratched my hand.

"Welcome, young Monsieur Morgat! Come in."

Out of the doorway stepped the pock-marked man who had visited the shop not so long before. He was wearing the same brown suit and the same old-fashioned overcoat, cut in military style. His tricorn was pushed back on his head and under it there was a brightly colored silk scarf.

"It's hotter than it was at Vera Cruz the day they hanged old George Matthew," he grumbled. "Come cool off with a long drink in my cabin. I'm glad to see you again. To tell the truth I had a notion you might come sniffing about this way. That's nothing against you. At your age curiosity is no fault, it's a necessity."

While he spoke in this playful vein I was able to take a good look at his gaunt frame and his hard, weatherbeaten, pock-marked face. But I couldn't size him up: he could have been an honest skipper or a villain of the first water. Most of the seafaring men I had known had the same hard look about them. The discipline that shaped their lives—whether they were at the giving end or the receiving—caused them to acquire a severe, almost cruel air.

"Sir, I accept your kind invitation. Perhaps you have something new to tell me. I admit that I should like to know more about certain events whose sequence and significance escape me."

"Well said, my boy. That's why I suggest the privacy of my cabin. Allow me to go first and show you the way."

The cramped cabin was choked with tobacco smoke. My host offered me a stool, he sat on the edge of the table.

"You've known Jean the Nightbird for some time, have you? 'Jailbird' might be a better name."

I told him briefly of how I had come to know the con-

110

vict and to take pity on him. But I said nothing about the flight to the coast in the company of Guénolé.

"I see," he said. "I don't know any more than you do. But he's a friend and he entrusted me with what he said was an important message. I've done what he asked, and now that we're alone I'd like you to acknowledge it."

"Gladly," I replied. "But I don't see how, except by turning up for the appointment."

"Jean the Nightbird is lying low. He's mistrustful. He won't come unless he has word in your hand telling him that I accomplished my mission. Is that clear?"

"Fairly clear . . ."

While I was reflecting he took a pen, inkwell, and sheet of paper out of a drawer in the table. He placed the paper in front of me, tested the point of the pen, and gazed up at the ceiling as if in search of inspiration.

"I'm not one of your literary blokes, but how about this? . . . *Tonight at midnight I'll be at the stone of Kéravel. I have something to tell you.*'"

I repeated the sentences to myself and saw nothing compromising about them. Then I picked up the pen and wrote them down on the sheet of paper.

"Now, sign," he said, looking over my shoulder. "Good. Now Jean the Nightbird will know that I delivered the message. He's a very fine fellow." With a sigh he folded the paper and slipped it into his overcoat pocket.

"Where is he?" I asked.

"That I don't know. When I see him it's in the fields near Plougastel; a go-between arranges the place of our meeting. But in the three weeks that we've been anchored here I've seen him no more than twice. He's in good health, that's all I can tell you."

111

With that he offered me a glass of barley syrup and cold water and himself gulped down a sizeable portion of rum. I set out for home, musing on the events of the afternoon and the adventure that lay just ahead. I was curious to see Jean the Nightbird and, above all, to hold in my hand the likeness of Petit-Radet.

Little did I know that by penning what seemed like two harmless sentences I had signed a death warrant.

11

Once more I alit, as it were, on the paving stones of the
Rue de Siam, which a night fog had made more slippery
than fishscales. The watchman had just gone by and I
could hear from a distance his melancholy, owl-like cry.
It was around eleven o'clock and the street was sleeping.
A few rays of light filtered through the shutters of the
"Firebrand," and I imagined Monsieur and Madame
Poder counting the money they had taken out of the
cashbox. I could feel the "borrowed" cutlass against my
thigh, and it lent me courage. The rank air of the street,
as I breathed it deeply into my lungs, acquired the intoxicating odor of war. Little by little I became accustomed to the weird shadows cast by the fitful and lugubrious light of the moon.

I skirted the walls, stopping after every few steps to listen for any unexpected noise. I did hear feeble sounds, without being able to place them. In the darkness, voices as well as lights were illusory. At a point not very far from home I heard muffled footsteps in an adjacent alley. Fortunately the moon was momentarily hidden by a mass of clouds and I crouched behind a gatepost. My instinct had done me good service, for a big man armed with a musket walked by, without my being able to see his face or the cut of his clothes. The footsteps came to a sudden stop and when I peered out from my hiding place I saw that he had come to a halt in front of our house and was gazing up at my window. It looked suspiciously as if he were keeping tabs on me. He was in no hurry, and took no precautions against being heard or seen. Indeed, he was humming loudly enough for me to hear him as he continued in the direction of the docks. I also had the impression that he was speaking to someone, but he was too far away for me to be sure.

With some misgivings I walked toward Kéravel. Some drunken sailors were fighting in front of a tavern, whose proprietor stood armed with a long skewer at the open door. Behind the sailors a group of rowdy women were calling shrilly for the police. In order to avoid trouble I decided to retrace my steps, returning to the Rue de Siam and walking along the docks and by the penitentiary. As far as I could judge from his retreating footsteps, this was the route followed by the stranger.

As I passed my own house I saw nothing unusual. My farther and Marianne must have been fast asleep in their country-style box beds. I went on toward the docks, carefully watching the entrances of the side streets and, above all, the gateways, where I was by now well aware that danger might be lurking. Fortunately there was plenty of time before I was due at my appointment. Without any cause for alarm I walked along the Penfeld and turned at the high wall of the penitentiary. At intervals along the top I saw a bayonet gleaming.

To the right was an alley bordered by tumbledown hovels. A freshly plastered house, painted bright red, stood out like a palace among them. This belonged to "Monsieur de Brest," the executioner (in everyday life Cotentin Fiburce), and the townsfolk generally gave it a wide berth, so that except for stray dogs and cats the alley was almost always deserted. As a matter of fact, few respectable people would have wandered among the sordid and crime-haunted streets of the Pont-Merdou section of the town. I myself was not exactly at ease, but pride was stronger than fear. God knows I was impulsive and even foolhardy, but once I had committed myself to an undertaking I saw it through. And so I pursued my way, taking the simple precaution of pushing the cutlass around to the front of my belt, where I could lay hands on it at a second's notice. Just in time, for a ghostly figure rose up out of the night and accosted me.

"Is that you, Yves-Marie?" said a breathless voice which I did not immediately recognize.

"Who goes there?" I retorted in soldierly fashion.

"Yves-Marie! It is I, Nicholas! How glad I am to have found you!" And grasping my arm he pulled me over to a wall whose buttresses hid us from view.

"Where are you off to, Yves-Marie? Mind, you don't have to tell me. But I'm here to warn you that you'd better go home . . . if there's still time."

"I'm going to an appointment with Jean the Night-bird."

"I know. And I know something else you don't know."

"What's that?"

"I just happened to be there . . . It's simple enough . . . Just listen . . ."

For a few moments he was silent while we both cocked an ear to make sure no one was near by. Then he went on, in a low but excited voice. "Above all, don't interrupt me. I had supper at the house of Monsieur de Forster. You know that I'm doing a portrait of his daughter. Afterward, I started home along the Esplanade. The evening was so fine that I paused to look down at the water and then decided to climb up by the Castle in order to see the moon rise over the harbor."

I started visibly at these last words.

"Never mind; it's nothing," I said reassuringly. "Go on."

"Well, I was climbing up the rocks that overhang the road circling the Castle when all of a sudden I realized that I wasn't alone. At once I made myself inconspicuous. Looking down, I saw two men on the dock, near a handsome schooner whose name I don't recall."

"The *Rose of Savannah?*"

"That may be it. Anyhow, they were talking together, and one of them said; 'Without that young idiot we'd be lost. We'd never lead the fish into the net. Now, thanks to his help the fish will be biting the bait. He knows the boy's writing, and that will bring him.' After that they lowered their voices and I couldn't hear as well, especially as the wind was blowing the other way. Finally I got a good look at one of the men. All I can tell you is that he was big as a mountain. The other fellow, whom I could hardly see, must have turned his head, because I heard him say, 'Above all, no noise. Those are the boss's

116

orders . . . A light touch!' He laughed loudly and added, 'A quick trip to hell with a spanking breeze behind!' That made the big man laugh also. 'I'll go see if young Morgat went to the meetingplace,' he said. 'Before joining the others I'll pass in front of the shop and throw a pebble up at his window.' The minute I heard your name I started running. I was sure I'd find you somewhere near the stone. For half an hour I've been looking."

"I must hurry now, to get there in time."

"My God, man, are you crazy? Didn't you hear what I told you? You'll get mixed up with a band of desperadoes . . ."

"I must go. Jean the Nightbird has to be warned that the pock-marked fellow is laying a trap for him. I have something to tell you, too, but later."

"I'll go with you then," said Nicolas somberly. And he moved his sword up and down in its leather sheath.

We started off in the direction of "Neptune's Wood," which was not far from the fateful stone, walking on opposite sides of the street in order to be ready for any surprise. Soon we came to an intersection, lit by a dusty lamp that barely allowed us to see the three alleys that came together. At the end of one of them another lamp was burning.

"That's it," I whispered. "That lamp hangs near 'Neptune's Wood.' It won't be long now."

"We're feeling our way like blind men," Nicolas complained. "Yves-Marie, I hope you won't regret this crazy adventure."

"We have to warn Jean the Nightbird. His life's at stake, and he may be an innocent man. But we won't get mixed up in any fighting. I have that much concern for the feelings of my father."

117

We advanced cautiously over the loose cobblestones and the shards of pottery that were mingled with them. Suddenly in the light of the lamp just ahead we saw a motionless figure. The man was making no effort to conceal his presence. He stood his ground, with his legs spread far apart and his hands in the pockets of a heavy coat.

"That must be he," I said to Nicolas.

In the distance we heard the mournful chant of the night watchman.

"Midnight," said Nicolas.

Without further precautions we stepped forward to meet Jean the Nightbird. Hearing our footsteps he came slowly to greet us, his hands still in his pockets. Then, with one of them, he took off his hat, and under it I saw the scarf worn by the pock-marked lieutenant of the *Rose of Savannah*. He gave us no time to get over our surprise, but with a calming gesture in the direction of Nicolas, who had grasped the hilt of his sword, he said, addressing me by name, "Young Monsieur Yves-Marie Morgat, it's time for you to be in bed. Go along home, you and your friend. No harm will come to you."

"And Jean the Nightbird?" I shouted angrily. "What have you done with him? You used me to get him into your hands."

"I used what I could, young gentleman. And, believe me, if I didn't have strict orders to handle you with gloves on I shouldn't waste any time on explanations. The wisest thing you can do is to go home and put this night out of your mind. That's my honest advice. Forget this night, both of you. As they say in the best circles, it's matter of life and death."

The blood went to my head and I was about to make

118

an indignant reply, when suddenly the air was rent by a loud cry, like that of a slaughtered beast. Nicolas flattened himself against the nearest wall, and I followed his example.

"I told you this was no place for you to be," said the pock-marked man coldly.

Shutters banged against a wall. There followed an oppressive silence, broken by loud cries from the direction of the new barracks of the regiment of Brest.

"Murder! Murder! Police!"

"Clear out, I tell you!" said the pock-marked man. "It's all over. And remember to keep your traps shut, for your own sake as well as ours."

Then, like a fox with the dogs at his heels, he turned tail and ran away. Nicolas was the first to recover the use of his voice.

"I told you so, you stubborn donkey! There's nothing to do but go home. We haven't much to be proud of. That swine treated us like a pair of schoolboys, and I must say we deserved it."

I was too enraged to listen to any good counsel. My ears still smarted from the humiliating words of the lieutenant of the *Rose of Savannah,* and my head buzzed with the cutting phrases with which I should have replied. Now it was too late, and I had to swallow my pride. But with all the stubbornness of my seafaring ancestors I managed to turn my shame to strength. Instead of running to safety, I drew myself up like a true Breton, more proudly than ever.

"There's where we must go," I said, pointing in the direction of the bloodcurdling cry. "If he's no more than wounded, perhaps we can help him."

Nicholas shrugged his shoulders.

"You can go on home," I said, cuttingly.

"Donkey!" he repeated. And without further words he followed me. Already I regretted my stupid insinuation. Now that he had made up his mind to see the thing through, however mistaken it might be, Nicolas did not bother to tread softly. As for me, I gripped the handle of my cutlass with convulsive anger.

"This way," I said.

We were in a narrow street leading to the Penfeld. The moon, now high in the sky, lit up a wheelbarrow half-overturned on a pile of sand and a beggar trying to sleep in its shelter. I shook him awake. "Didn't you hear a loud noise a few minutes ago?" I asked. Then I repeated the question in Breton dialect.

The beggar struggled to his feet. His face was ravaged by leprosy, and he stared at me out of one enormous, malicious, fish-eye. "There," he said, pointing to the right, and lay down again under the wheelbarrow.

After we had gone a short way in the direction in which he had pointed, we saw a spot of dark-red, almost black, liquid—obviously blood—on the street and splotches of the same on a door. We searched the immediate surroundings without finding any further traces of the crime whose echoes had pierced our ears not long before.

"They must have taken the body away," I said.

"Probably not very far," was Nicolas's answer. And in reponse to my questioning look he imitated the beggar's gesture and pointed toward the Penfeld. "There."

It was beginning to grow light and there was not much time for me to get home unseen. We made for the Rue de Siam, and Nicolas stood guard while I climbed up the rain pipe. When he saw me push back the half-open shutter he went away. Leaning out the window I watched him walk to the end of the street and safely enter his own house.

I shut the window, took off my coat, jacket, waistcoat, and shirt and washed my face in cold water. Immediately I felt purified. The cutlass was still hanging from my belt. I unbuckled it and threw it on the bed. There was no question of sleeping. I opened the window and looked out, first at the sky and then at the docks. All was calm. Gradually the pink and green light of dawn dispelled the shadows of the night.

I was still perturbed, and uncertain as to what to do. I knew that the inhuman cry in the night had announced the death of Jean the Nightbird, lured to destruction by a note written in my own hand. What a scurvy trick the men from the *Rose of Savannah* had played upon me! But my feeling of humiliation and resentment did not blind me to the fact that a monstrous crime weighed upon my shoulders. The sad results of my two escapades were quite obvious, and to clear my conscience I decided to make a clean breast of the whole thing to my father. I was about to turn the knob of his door when it occurred to me that I might better seek first the advice of Mr. Burns. He alone could give me some comfort and help me to word my confession.

The church bell rang, and I bent my head to pray with all my heart for the soul of Jean the Nightbird. The painted figures on my shelves were poignant reminders of the skill of his gnarled hands.

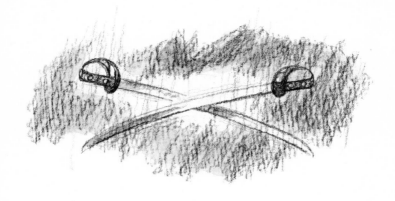

12

No one answered Madame Le Meur's bell, and the shutters of Mr. Burns's window were closed. I was about to go back to Brest when at the end of the street I saw the widow herself. I waited at the door to ask for news of her tenant.

"Are you sure he's not there?" she asked me. "Did you call him? He may be still asleep. Shall I wake him up?"

"Oh no, don't wake him. I'll come back around four o'clock this afternoon. When you see him, just tell him that I was here and that I'll be back later. I want to ask his advice."

After she had promised to give Mr. Burns my message,

I started home by way of the bridge and Kéravel. I was anxious to see if there were any traces of the murder beyond those Nicholas and I had seen the night before. In broad daylight I retraced the itinerary we had followed in the darkness, from the silent "Neptune's Wood" to the moss-covered stone and the corner where the beggar had been sleeping. Every trace of blood had been absorbed by the ground, and as for the wall, it bore signs of recent scrubbing. The early morning sun had not yet beat upon it, and the surface was still damp.

When I got back to the house I applied myself, without enthusiasm, to my geography. I was still anxious to talk to my father, but determined to consult Mr. Burns first. In the course of this Friday morning other happenings increased my uneasiness. Toward noon an ill-shaven but neatly dressed young man came into the shop and asked my father if he had any dealings with the *Rose of Savannah*. Had the captain, a certain Mathieu Tubeuf of Dieppe, bought hardware and tinned beef from us?

"I've never laid eyes on him," said my father, "nor have I sold anything to the members of his crew."

"Forgive the disturbance, sir," said the young man. "I just wanted to know."

"A copper," said my father, after the strange visitor had left. "Why in the world was he so curious about that ship? Frankly, I don't understand."

I was tempted to tell him of the strange scene I had witnessed on the deck of the schooner and of the voice —which for a moment had seemed to me to resemble that of Mr. Burns—of the man who had passed by me as I was hiding just off the path leading up to the Castle. But this would have meant recounting the events of the preceding night and so I held my tongue.

Later, when I came down from several hours of distracted reading in my room, my father told me that the pock-marked customer of the day before had been hanging about the door, pretending to be interested in the contents of the window.

"I know now who he is, father," I said excitedly. "He's an officer from the *Rose of Savannah*. I feel there's danger in the air, and perhaps a threat to Mr. Burns. We must warn him . . . if it isn't too late. Isn't it strange that he hasn't been around?"

"True; we haven't seen him for several days. Let me see . . . today's Friday . . ."

Brusquely my father pushed his wig back on his head, a sure sign of agitation.

"Go over to Recouvrance, Yves-Marie, and find out how he is. He may be ill. No, you mind the shop and I'll go there myself."

Involuntarily I made a gesture of discomfiture.

"What's that?" said my father. "You've been out too much lately. A quiet afternoon won't do you any harm."

"Very true," put in Marianne. "Look at the boy's pale face! He's as white as a Roscoff turnip!"

My father picked up his hat and cane, and Marianne went upstairs to turn down the beds. I pressed my nose to the windowpane and gazed disconsolately at the street. My attention was caught by some marching soldiers. Opening the door I saw a company of a hundred or so fusiliers of the Brest regiment, with white leather straps crossed over their shoulders, cartridge pouches at their belts, and knapsacks on their backs. They were led by their lieutenant Monsieur Rateau, who carried a gun on his shoulder, and followed by a drummer boy with a drum in the place of the knapsack. They were marching

125

toward the docks, a troop of boys at their heels. Among these I recognized Yannik, the fourteen-year-old son of Kenavo Maheu, the carpenter, who often ran errands for my father.

"What's going on?" I called out to him.

He pointed excitedly in the direction of the Castle.

"Tell me about it later!" I shouted, and he nodded to show that he had heard me.

An hour later my father came back, with a worried look on his face and the news that Mr. Burns was not there; indeed, his landlady had not seen him all day. He sighed, took off his coat and went back to work without saying anything further.

As for me, it was all I could do to contain myself. I longed to join Yannik and his friends, but my father seemed to be in no mood to let me go out. I too sighed, and sat down with a book near the window, hoping to catch Yannik when he returned. It was four o'clock, and I thought he had forgotten all about me, when I heard the clatter of his wooden shoes. With a single bound I was out on the street. "Well, then?" I asked impatiently.

"They boarded the *Rose of Savannah*," he told me. "The docks are crowded with people. There's a company of the Karrer regiment beside the fusiliers of our own, and all the local constabulary. The coast guards are watching the shore between Portzic and Lanninon. It seems that the *Rose of Savannah* is a pirate craft disguised as a merchantman; an officer and part of the crew have been arrested, and the others have fled. They stole a boat on the Aberwrach and put out to sea . . ."

"In the direction of the Scilly Islands," said one of the other boys who had now joined him.

"That nobody knows. But the whole town's in turmoil.

126

The prisoners will be hauled before the court and flogged on the Esplanade."

"And they've sighted a drowned man in the water," said the other. "The body is floating out with the tide."

"That's true," said Yannik. "I must go back in a hurry, If I go around by Recouvrance I'll be just in time to see them haul it ashore."

The whole band turned tail, and there was a stampede of wooden shoes on the paving stones. I could restrain myself no longer. Grabbing my hat from inside the door I rushed after them, calling out an "I'll be back soon," which left no time for an answer. Little groups of townsmen—old and young—were streaming over the bridge and toward the mouth of the river. I looked up at Madame Le Meur's house and saw that Mr. Burns's shutters were still closed. The good lady herself was in the garden.

"He's still away," she called out. "In fact, he doesn't seem to have slept in his bed last night."

As I went down a terraced alley leading to the sea I saw four men looking out over the water with their hands cupped above their eyes to protect them from the blinding sun. They were fishermen.

"They've got him," said one. "Jean-Pierre's boathook did the job."

And they went on down the steps, pushing aside the honeysuckle branches that almost barred the narrow alley. I followed hard on their heels all the way to a stony beach where some thirty people, most of them children, were waiting. A constable was keeping them at a respectful distance from a rowboat some fishermen were hauling up onto the shore. When I joined the onlookers, Yannik among them, the drowned man's corpse was already laid on a stretcher and covered by a tarpaulin.

"Did you get a look at him?" I asked Yannik.

"I saw him as clearly as I see you. He's that convict, Jean the Nightbird, who escaped a few months ago from the penitentiary. I used to run into him every morning with the street-sweeping squad."

"Poor fellow, he killed himself!" exclaimed a woman who sold fish in the marketplace.

"Killed himself, you say?" a sailor interrupted mockingly. "With the aid of a good friend who put a knife between his shoulders!"

"One convict the less, that's all," said a fellow who might have been a merchant. "A case hardly worth investigating. In those circles dog eats dog."

Three more constables arrived on the scene, and two fishermen took hold of the stretcher and carried it joltingly up to Recouvrance. Along with Yannik I followed the little procession.

This sight left an indelible mark upon my mind. What happened afterward was on a larger scale and far more terrifying, but many of the details I have forgotten. Yet, even today, when I am a seasoned artillery officer, I can see one of Jean the Nightbird's feet sticking out from under the tarpaulin as vividly as if it were still before me.

The stretcher, escorted by the constables, was carried into the courtyard of the penitentiary, whose gate opened onto the parade ground of the Karrer regiment. The gate swung shut, and the hangers-on were left outside, where they stayed for at least a quarter of an hour, discussing what they had seen. No one could doubt that there had been foul play. The fishermen had seen the knife with their own eyes—an Oriental blade, whose wooden handle was oramented with silver filigree.

"That's a signature to the crime," said one of the men

from Plougastel. "The signature of a pirate."

"Petit-Radet," put in another.

"That may well be. Petit-Radet or one of his ilk. It's the language of the black flag."

Little by little the group dispersed. The fishermen went into a café, and I made my way home, anxious to tell the story to my father and Marianne. Nicolas too, I hoped, would have come by this time to pay me a visit. We had yet to discuss our common experience of the night before.

"Jesus save us! Jesus save us!" my father murmured as I breathlessly told him what I had seen.

In my mind, nothing connected Mr. Jerome Burns with this last fatal event. As for the *Rose of Savannah*, I was not surprised that it should have turned out to have such a lurid character. From the very beginning this mysterious, half-abandoned schooner had aroused my suspicions. I thought back to the man with the pock-marked face, now revealed to be a member of a pirate crew. What affected me most was the sight of Jean the Nightbird's dead body. Suddenly my father said. "Run over to Recouvrance and find out if Mr. Burns is there. If, as I imagine, he has returned, ask him to come here for supper. We'll tell him the whole story." And, after a moment of reflection, he added, "If he doesn't know it already . . ."

"But Father, when I went by the house just now his shutters were closed."

"Never mind," said my father, with unaccustomed brusqueness. "You'd better go see. He may have come back by now and be sleeping. All these goings-on in town and along the coast are disquieting. It's a bad business, and I don't like it."

129

I had reasons of my own not to like it, either, but this my father did not know.

Mr. Burns's shutters were, as I had expected, still closed. I went through the garden gate and knocked at the front door. Madame Le Meur let me in and took me back to the kitchen, where she was busy peeling vegetables. Her black cat sat on a stool, surveying the operation with his round, green eyes.

"You want news of Mr. Burns, of course," said Madame Le Meur, offering me a chair. "But I know no more than you. His things are in disorder, but they're all there —his books on the tables and his clothes in the wardrobe —as if he expected to return. He took nothing with him except the new suit he was wearing. So he'll be back . . . at least I hope so, for things are no longer easy for me. I need glasses . . . I have here a pair sent me by my older sister, but they must be too strong, because everything seems indistinct, and . . ."

"Couldn't we go up to Mr. Burns's room together?" I interrupted. "He may have left a note for me."

"Certainly. You go first. I haven't touched a thing."

I entered the room, with Madame Le Meur behind me. The room, was, indeed, in disorder, and this made me think that Mr. Burns's departure had been sudden and hurried. There was an atmosphere of alarm, and I could hear my father saying, "I don't like it." My first glance was at the mantelpiece, but there was no note awaiting me. The pistols were gone and a sword was missing from the wall, leaving the imprint of its sheath behind. I knew that Mr. Burns was law abiding and never carried a weapon, even at night. The absence of the pistols and sword was a bad omen, but I did not say so to Madame Le Meur.

"It's true that he left everything in disorder, but, as you say, that means he'll be back. His trunk and his sea chest are still in the corner. As soon as he comes tell him that my father and I are anxious to see him and hope that he will come to supper."

"Certainly, young gentleman. I shan't fail."

I went home not only worried but also disappointed. I had counted on confessing my recent imprudence to Mr. Burns and having the benefit of his advice.

"What's your theory about our friend's absence?" my father asked me.

I pursed my lips and shrugged my shoulders. My father looked out at the new sign over the door, which was creaking in the evening breeze. Then he returned to behind the counter. "May the anchor of mercy protect those whom we hold dear!" he said with a sigh.

In the continued absence of our friend the evening meal was a sad one. Sitting opposite each other, we munched our bread in silence, each of us lost in his own preoccupations and premonitions.

"Tomorrow is Saturday," I said at last. "I'll ask about him in the town.

"Very good," said my father. "You'll enquire around town, and in the afternoon we'll go to the 'Firebrand.' There we're sure to have some news."

During the last fortnight we had had few visits from our friends. Pillawer was out covering the country marketplaces, Kilvinec was fishing off the Green Islands, old Goas was in bed with a high fever, and Monsieur de Pinville had gone to Paramé to see his son, who was a lieutenant in the regiment of La Fère.

My father was a sociable man and this lack of company weighed upon him. But what weighed most heavily was the absence of Mr. Burns. In the past months he had become a part of our life, almost a member of the family. His good humor, honesty, and lightly worn erudition had given him a sure place in our affections. Now we were afraid that he had suffered some misfortune. And the element of uncertainty added to our fear.

Digwener of Couesnon, the master of the *Rose-de-Marie,* came every week to bring us some fish, usually from the mouth of the Elorn. But he hardly knew Mr. Burns and had nothing to tell us. Outside of my father Mr. Burns had no intimate friends. In spite of his kindliness he was a taciturn man; like many old sea dogs he said little about the past. It had often occurred to me that the name *Mercy,* which he had given to his ship, had a secret significance and that behind it there lay a long story. All I knew, of course, was that he had held her command. On the day when we first sighted the *Rose of Savannah* I had been deeply touched by this revelation.

13

The first thing we saw when we walked into the "Fire-brand" was the angry look on the face of Monsieur Poder, who was confiding his woes to a sympathetic customer.

"The little slut cleared out at night, with all her belongings packed in a little trunk lent her by my soft-hearted wife. Hand-painted it was, and so artistically you'd have sworn the flowers were real. We'd had it ever since we were married, and now God knows if we'll ever see it again. We're in a real fix, besides. It isn't easy to train a girl to serve guests as distinguished as ours."

"Who's that?" my father asked him.

"Manon. She stole away like a thief."

"Too bad," said my father politely, going to join Monsieur de Pinville, who had returned the evening before and was setting up the chessboard in expectation of his arrival.

My father at once repeated the news. "It seems that young Manon is missing."

"Yes," said Monsieur de Pinville, joining in his laughter. "She has shaken the dust of the 'Firebrand' from her feet, and our host is brokenhearted."

"He's brokenhearted over the loss of a trunk."

"That may be," said Monsieur de Pinville with a sly wink.

"May I serve you some coffee, Monsieur Morgat?" asked Monsieur Poder.

"Just as usual," said my father. "And don't worry. She'll be back."

"Of course she'll be back," put in an elderly officer who came to the café to play backgammon. "You can put that in your pipe and smoke it!"

I didn't take the departure of Manon de Gwened so lightly. Although, once more, I couldn't make any logical deduction from this apparently trivial event, it added a new element to my worries. The accumulation of coincidences was more than I could deal with. As I sat a little to one side and behind my father my imagination ran wild. I felt like a spider caught in its own web, or rather in a web woven by mysterious enemies. Sounds and figures danced around me, but I could not identify them. In the chain of events there were persons I knew, but they were mere puppets, and others, whom I did not know, were pulling the strings. This latest bit of news seemed to me inextricably woven with the absence of Mr. Burns, the raid on the *Rose of Savannah,* and the violent death of Jean the Nightbird. Not to mention the unknown and relatively unimportant fate of such sordid minor figures as Guénolé, Thomas the Souse, Raspberry, and Ninon Glao, all of them connected in one way or another with the dark alleys and underworld of Kéravel.

What was the role of Manon de Gwened, whom I knew only as a girl with melting eyes, an upturned nose, a childish mouth, and honey-colored hair? I wondered if perhaps Nicolas, who had been flirting with her all these past months, might have a clue. But just as I was turning this possibility over in my mind he dispelled my suspicions by walking into the room, every inch the innocent and despairing lover. Only Friday evening, before he had gone to search for me in Kéravel, she had waited upon him with her usual endearing laugh and her usual teasing. Now he gulped down a glass of rum, with as tragic an air as if she had deceived him. Fortunately, from the glances he shot at the new waitress, a pretty brunette, I judged that Nicolas's despair would not last forever. Actually I, without being in love with Manon, was perhaps the more affected by her departure. But this was because I was more deeply involved in the mysterious and almost vulgarly melodramatic events that were shaking the town. More than ever I felt that the secret of my reckless participation in them was too heavy for me to bear.

Around us the backgammon players were throwing their dice violently on the board. Nicolas and I morosely followed their moves, gradually finding solace in the players' enthusiasm and the cool comfort of the airy room. I was roused from my melancholy torpor by the voice of my father saying, "By Saint Ives! Here he is in person!"

And there he was, indeed, as smiling and amiable as

ever, wiping the perspiration from his forehead as he walked toward us. I literally jumped out of my chair. "Mr. Burns!" I shouted.

"Hello there, Little Morgat! Hello, Nicolas!"

"For the second time we've missed you like the very devil!" my father exclaimed. "Yves-Marie has been trotting about looking for you like a puppy. And the 'Anchor of Mercy' hasn't been the same without you."

Mr. Burns seemed to appreciate the warmth of our welcome. He smiled broadly as he sat down, and responded with the simple words, "My good friends . . ." Then, with one hand on his knees he scrutinized the progress of the game.

"Manon de Gwened has run away," I told him.

"What? Our charming Manon? Is it true, Monsieur Poder, that you've lost this treasure?"

"The little slut! Don't mention her name!"

"There's the question of a trunk, too," I said maliciously.

"A trunk? What trunk?"

I filled in the story.

"By George!" Mr. Burns exclaimed. "If it weren't that our host might misinterpret my action, I'd offer to pay him for the trunk. But a man of my age shouldn't get involved in the affairs of a young girl."

"You must join us for supper," said my father, who had just lost the game.

Mr. Burns accepted the invitation with unusual alacrity. "Gladly, Jean-Sébastien Morgat. It will do me good to be in your company. I've been away on a piece of business which have given me some trouble."

"Is there any way I can help you?" asked my father.

"Alas, no. The trouble is caused by a friend of days

gone by. Mind, little Morgat, it's no joke when the events of your youth return to haunt you in your old age. Don't contract too many obligations. The time may come when it is difficult to repay."

Mr. Burns liked to cite, even if somewhat elliptically, his own experiences and to draw a moral from them. But although his manner was joking there was an overtone of melancholy in his words.

We walked home slowly, breathing in the wind-blown fragrance of the gardens of Lanninon. A gang of boys from the Seven Saints district, armed with sticks and slings, was gathering for an expedition against a similar gang from Recouvrance. The Rue de Siam was, in these days, particularly animated. Troops continued to pour through the town and sometimes to lodge there on their way either to Paramé or the other camp near Bayeux, in Normandy. Now the street presented a panorama of uniforms—the white of the infantry, the blue of the cavalry and the green of the dragoons. My eye was caught, of course, by the dark blue with red trimmings of the artillery. Heavy cannons were lined up along the Cours d'Ajot and a sentinel stood guard, with a bayonet attached to the barrel of his gun.

By now we knew all too well the meaning of such activity. War was at hand and our coastline was subject to attack. The fishermen among our customers were watching out anxiously for English ships, and merchantmen were unloading their cargoes in the safer ports of La Rochelle and Bordeaux. The wreckers, such as Guénolé, found no more victims.

Only our friend Digwener, the master of the *Rose-de-Marie,* had the courage to fish far out at sea, between Concarneau and the Bay of Biscay, reaping a high price for his catch from the merchants of Landerneau, Landi-visiau, and Sizun. It was Digwener that brought us news of the coastal islands. Petit-Radet had not been seen either at Groix or at Ouessant. A frigate, armed with twelve cannons, was still sweeping the seas and the coast guards continued to scour the moors, searching for him.

"They're a strange lot, Petit-Radet and his fellows," said Mr. Burns at the table. "Of course, they outrage our most sacred principles. But their very recklessness has a certain fascination."

"I see what you mean," said my father. "But why, of all professions, did they have to choose that of crime?"

"You may well ask. But life presents us with mysterious choices. We choose a path, and when we perceive its dangers it may be too late to retreat." And, turning to me, he added, "There's no turning back, Little Morgat. This is a law of nature, and don't you forget it. When I tell you that adventure is a snare and a delusion, it's with forty years of experience behind me. I was twelve years old when I first put out to sea. Rough, often cruel men taught me their code. It's only by God's good grace I managed to save my soul and preserve my reason."

"How right you are!" sighed my father.

"Go to war, that's my advice," said Mr. Burns. "War is cruel enough, God knows, but it's not without honor."

"The war will be over," I said ruefully, "before I win my commission."

"There's no end to war," said Mr. Burns, joining in my father's laugher. "One fine day you'll hear the cannons speak. And you'll be fighting for rather than against the law."

He went on to enquire about how I was spending the

summer. I was lucky, he said, to be entering the army just at the time when Monsieur de Gribeauval and Monsieur de Vallières were modernizing the weapons of the artillery. And he expatiated on the merits of the regulation rifle with which the army was to be equipped the following year.

The evening passed quickly, and shortly before ten o'clock Mr. Burns left for home. I went to bed much easier in my mind. Now that Mr. Burns was back things would improve. I would go see him tomorrow and in the privacy of his own room unburden myself of my story. He alone could tell me whether to keep the whole affair to myself or to make a clean breast of it to my father. And if he advised silence, the responsibility would not be mine alone.

Mr. Burns himself was the first to lead the way to a discussion of the events that had so long harassed me. He was sitting in his armchair, wearing a dressing gown with a floral design and smoking his pipe. Through the wide-open window came the smell of salt water and new ropes and the sound of a whistle blown by the overseer of a gang of convicts engaged in transporting boards to a nearby drydock.

"Curious, the sudden eclipse of Manon," he observed. "I didn't think she was the kind of a girl to lose her head."

"I don't think she did lose it. She knows what's what, and I believe the whole thing was carefully planned."

"Would you call it a kidnapping?"

"I don't know. I'm quite at sea."

"Tell me what went on while I was away. You know, I find you greatly changed, Little Morgat. You're like a rudderless ship, as if you were about to drop the anchor

139

of mercy. That's the last anchor, and it mustn't give way. If the storm breaks it, you'll be adrift. But as long as I'm here that shan't happen, I promise you . . . I solemnly swear it."

Then, with my head bowed and my arms hanging between my legs, I told him the whole story of my indiscretions, from the flight with Jean the Nightbird, Raspberry, and Guénolé to the knifing of Jean, whose death cry still rang in my ears. I told of the *Rose of Savannah,* the pock-marked lieutenant and the mysterious individual who rushed by me on the path to the Castle. But I was reluctant to admit that for a moment I had fancied I recognized this individual's voice.

"You never saw him again?" asked Mr. Burns, filling his pipe.

"No."

"And did he awaken any train of memories, any association of images? When our nerves are on edge such things are apt to float through the mind."

"No . . . That is, there was something familiar about his voice, as if it belonged to someone I know . . . But only for a second, not long enough to be of any importance . . ."

"The voice of Goas? Jean the Nightbird? Your friend Nicolas?"

"No, none of these. To tell the truth, it was closer to yours. But that just shows how my ears deceived me. You had gone to Quimper at the time, as I remember."

Mr. Burns nodded. He was puffing peacefully at his pipe, pausing at intervals to remove the red-tipped white-clay stem from his mouth and blow a stream of bitter-smelling smoke toward the ceiling. The smoke-laden air made me feel sleepy. As I sat there, staring at my shoe

140

buckles, Mr. Burns rose and began to pace up and down the room. Brusquely he stopped in front of me and pointed the pipe stem at my chest.

"You did well to confide in me, Little Morgat," he said. "You got yourself mixed up with something that's too much for you to handle alone. For the time being, say nothing to your father. He'd only be upset. You're guilty of nothing more than foolhardiness. And I, for one, can't blame you for that. When I was twelve years old I ran away to sea . . . Meanwhile, promise me that you won't try to dig further into the secrets of this band of rascals. Petit-Radet is somehow back of it all. Too bad that Jean the Nightbird's statuette of him is lost. If you ask me, that's what they were after."

"I wonder if the pock-marked lieutenant of the *Rose of Savannah* may not be he."

"That's most unlikely. Smallpox isn't all that frequent, and if such a notorious fellow as Petit-Radet were marked by it, the word would have gotten around."

"Anyhow, Mr. Burns, I promise you that I'll meddle no more in other people's business. Only what about Manon?"

"Leave Manon to her fate. It wouldn't surprise me if she'd run off with one of the crew of the *Rose of Savannah*. This is a small town, and everything is bound to hang together. You've seen that for yourself."

Mr. Burns's words were so wise that I could not but approve them. His calm assurance restored my peace of mind, and I felt infinitely better than I had an hour before.

"Everything will be all right, Little Morgat," he concluded. "You're waking up from a bad dream. At your age one doesn't detect evil, and the false innocence of

Jean the Nightbird took you in. Let it be a lesson to you. You can count yourself blessed if, at this early age, you learn to beware of your fellowman."

"Are men so incomprehensible, then?" I queried.

"You have many disillusionments still ahead of you, Little Morgat," said Mr. Burns, without giving my question a direct answer.

14

Nothing worthy of note happened during the last week
of the month of July. Soldiers marched interminably
through the town. In the countryside they were feared for
all the world like emissaries of the devil, because of the
number of ducks and geese that disappeared in their train.
Every regiment had its camp followers, a motley crew of
grooms, women, and children—all of them adept at
thievery and given to bad language. A squadron of Pied-
montese cavalry, with royal-blue jackets and yellow-
trimmed coats, was famous for its brutal manners and
depredations. Finally, disciplinary measures were taken
and order was restored.

My chief amusement was to take long daily walks on

the road to Rennes, in the company of either Mr. Burns or Nicolas. The latter continued to talk about Manon de Gwened. According to him, she wasn't worth the rope it would take to hang her. She was a real slut, and the amiability she had displayed at the "Firebrand" was just one of the tricks of her trade.

"Actually she's a spy!" he shouted. "She's in the enemy's pay."

"So you really think so? I don't."

"You're as thickheaded as an artilleryman!" Nicolas shouted. "You go around with your head in the air, bestowing blessings, but without seeing what's in front of your nose. Manon has always dabbled in reading English books. Just ask Goas or Mr. Burns, and see what they have to say. She's feeding the enemy information about the movement of our troops. King George's spies are all over the place. Lord Bute pays well. The officers of the *Néère* were talking among themselves about Manon just the other night, at the 'Firebrand.' "

"I can't believe she's a spy. That's only gossip . . ."

"Gossip? Are you sure? And what if I told you that the police commissioner had dropped in on Poder last Monday morning?"

"The police commissioner?"

"Yes, my boy. The commissioner with his snuffbox, and Lanceleau, his lieutenant, with his little black notebook, and four stout men to escort them."

"You mean that Poder is involved in the affair?"

"Poder's not responsible for the misdeeds of Manon. They went simply to find out what he knew about her. Obviously there's some reason for their curiosity."

"Well, I'll be . . ."

There was really nothing I could say, and we went on

144

to talk of other things. A group of raw recruits, led by an elderly officer on a lame nag, caught our attention. Apparently they were coming straight from home, since they were wearing civilian clothes and carrying their belongings on their shoulders. They dragged their feet and had disconsolate expressions, although one of them, who was followed by a white dog, all skin and bones, sang in a thin unconvincing voice:

> *I don't miss my father and mother,*
> *I don't miss my sister and brother,*
> *I tell you I've got a girl . . .*

The last straggling member of the group was weeping like a newly weaned calf. They disappeared, finally, beyond a clump of trees, but the dust kicked up by their heels made us sneeze for several minutes after.

In the town, Manon's name was on everyone's lips. People normally sensible enough had succumbed to war hysteria; under every bush they saw an agent of George III or of the police. We lived in an atmosphere of feverish excitement, which lent a heightened interest to the petty events of every day.

The day after my talk with Nicolas I ran into the commissioner of police, his lieutenant, and several men just outside our door.

"I'm lucky to find you, young Monsieur Morgat," said the commissioner. "That means I can kill two birds with one stone."

I went with the visitor into the shop. My father greeted him amiably enough, but with imperceptible impatience, because he was reluctant to leave his work. The commissioner had come, of course, to enquire about Manon. By

now her notoriety exceeded that of Isabelle du Faou, the seventeenth-century lady bandit whose ghost haunted many a late evening revel.

"You must excuse me, Monsieur Morgat, but we're conducting an investigation. The local force and the mounted police of the provost marshal are searching the town and its environs. But we haven't been able to put our finger on anything. Monsieur Poder's habitués know the girl all right, but they have very little concrete information about her."

"And is it so serious a matter?" enquired my father.

"Yes, it is. We are practically sure that the girl is an accomplice and perhaps also the mistress of Petit-Radet. It looks more and more as if he were in the neighborhood and in English pay. The eventual purpose would be the destruction of the squadron of ships that is presently being outfitted in our shipyards."

"What? Is it possible?" my father exclaimed.

"Anything seems possible when you belong to the police, Monsieur Morgat. But we don't believe everything we hear. At present we're simply checking up on a multitude of rumors."

Just then the tall figure of Mr. Burns appeared through the panes of the front window. He half opened the door, took off his tricorn hat, and stuck his kindly face with the fleshy, slightly split nose through the crack to bid us good day. "Excuse me," he said in a slightly singsong voice when he saw that we had a visitor. "I didn't mean to interrupt you."

"You're not interrupting," my father assured him. "We're only talking to the commissioner. Come right in."

"I have an errand to do down the street," said Mr. Burns. "I'll be back in a quarter of an hour."

147

"Who is that gentleman?" the commissioner asked. "I don't think I've seen him before."

"He's a retired navy surgeon who lives at Recouvrance."

"I see . . . Well, Monsieur Morgat, I needn't keep you any longer. I thank you for your courtesy."

But when he opened the door he exclaimed: "What? My men didn't wait?"

"No," I said, "they left five minutes ago. They must have had the notion that you would soon follow."

"Perhaps so," said the commissioner disgustedly, "but I'll wager that good-for-nothing Lanceleau has gone to wet his whistle." And he trotted down the street toward the docks, looking like a gray mouse with a rumpled white collar.

A few minutes later Mr. Burns came back from his errand, rubbing his hands together as he always did when he was in a good humor. First he asked for a week's supply of Puerto Rico tobacco. "How goes it, Yves-Marie? Still engrossed by your deadly ballistics?"

I smiled, and my father answered for me. "He's not really working. I only hope that the artillery school pulls him out of his daydreams and his bad company."

"But the boy has nothing to do with the affair of the perfidious Manon."

"You know about her?" asked my father.

"Certainly. For a week the commissioner's been questioning passers-by. He operates with all the subtlety of a goldfish in an aquarium. The provost marshal's office is on the alert too, and making enquiries among the troops. Next we shall see the constabulary."

"The commissioner asked me your name," my father told him.

"Curiosity is the virtue of his profession. What's *his* name, by the way?"

"Ask our walking encyclopaedia!" my father said with a laugh.

"Duglois," I answered, "Barnabé Duglois. He's a former sergeant of the king's bodyguard, from Paris, obviously."

"Then he's bound to be bright," said Mr. Burns good-naturedly. "Here's hoping he rids us of Petit-Radet, and Manon too, since she's said to be his mistress. Meanwhile, for a pastime closer to nature, I invite your father and yourself to a picnic luncheon tomorrow. Madame Le Meur will prepare it. Tomorrow is Sunday, and ship chandlers, like other good Christians, respect the Lord's day by closing their shops. Don't say no, Morgat, or I shall be very unhappy! By the way, I've ordered a carriage to take us and our provisions to a wooded spot with a view over the strait."

"That's the kind of a day I like!" I exclaimed, tossing my arms up in the air.

"The wise child!" said Mr. Burns genially. "Wiser than his father!"

The vehicle that took us to Portzic was a coach with leather curtains, which the driver had raised in order that we might enjoy the sea breeze. The coach was actually on its last legs; it was only by a miracle that it still held together. But the road was not too long and we had two stout horses.

The weather contributed to the perfection of the day. The sun was shining brightly, but a cool breeze from the north prevented it from being too hot. I sat beside young Hervé, on the driver's box, while my father and Mr.

Burns rode inside with the picnic paraphernalia.

After an hour's climb, part of which we made by foot in order to rest the horses, we came to the pine grove Mr. Burns had baptized "the nature-lover's meetingplace." It was indeed an agreeable spot. The shade of the trees was sufficient to protect us from the sun without eclipsing the view of the strait below. Here we laid a cloth on the ground and unpacked the baskets. Madame Le Meur's picnic fare was succulent and abundant, for Mr. Burns was both a discriminating and a heavy eater. My father had brought a basket prepared by Marianne, which contained a bottle of old port and some cakes she knew were to the taste of our host and friend. Every dish was presented with such art as to stimulate an already lively appetite, and we clapped our hands in approval. Young Hervé had his share of the meal, but on the driver's box, for it seemed unlikely that his commerce with horses had made him able to contribute to even the most rustic philosophical discussion.

My father drank his port to the health of Jean-Jacques Rousseau and Mr. Burns raised his glass to the glory of Monsieur de Buffon. As for me, my toast was to the cadets of the royal artillery school of Metz.

The good food, the sparkling cider that followed the port, and the good conversation made this picnic one of the happiest memories of my youth. Through the slender pines and twisted dwarf oaks we could glimpse the calm waters of the strait. Fishing boats were sailing out to cast their nets just off the coast, since fear of the English prevented them from going any farther. A navy store ship was maneuvering to dock at the Spanish Dike. Far away, in the direction of Camaret, we heard a cannon.

"Nothing serious," said Mr. Burns, listening intently. "Just gunnery exercises, with old barges for targets." A little later he remarked, "Yves-Marie is growing up. He's no longer running after adventure, like a chicken chasing a butterfly."

"That's largely on account of your good advice," said my father. "Like all the young he has moments of being overexcited. The development of the mind is even more despotic than the development of the body."

"At his age I was exactly the same," said Mr. Burns, patting my shoulder. I felt the emotion beneath these words, although he at once made light of it. "An honorable and courageous officer, an officer loyal to king and country, that's what you'll be, my boy. And someday, when you're a gray-haired officer, you'll remember my tutoring."

"I'll remember that and a great many other things," I told him. "Among them the oath I took on the day when we put up a new sign over our shop in your honor."

"What a boy you are, Little Morgat! But I don't remember your taking any oath on that occasion."

"I did, but to myself."

When it was time to go home we had to wake up young Hervé, who was snoring on the box, his face as red as a side of raw beef. Slowly we went down the dusty, uneven roads to the town. As we passed the docks we saw a great crowd of people. "They're probably waiting for some soldiers to march by," said Mr. Burns.

The coach made its way through the crowd to the accompaniment of bland imprecations and flourishings of the whip on the part of our youthful driver.

"What's going on?" said my father, looking out the window. "Is it a riot?" And catching sight of a young clerk whom he knew he called out, "What's it all about, Louis?"

"Good evening, Monsieur Morgat. You don't know? Monsieur Duglois, the commissioner of police, was assassinated in his bed early this morning. They've just found the body."

"What a scandal!" my father exclaimed indignantly. "Nothing of the kind has ever happened in our town before."

When we got out at "The Anchor of Mercy" it was around seven o'clock. The whole street was in turmoil. In front of the Feuneun pancake house and various shops and cafés, little knots of people were discussing the murder.

"Let's go have a glass of wine at the 'Firebrand,' " said Mr. Burns. "There we'll get the latest news of the crime, if crime it was."

At the "Firebrand" the excitement was more restrained but none the less strong. The click of the dice was less loud than the buzz of conversation.

"Duglois had a knife planted between his shoulders," Monsieur de Pinville told my father.

"His lieutenant found him around noon," put in Monsieur Poder. "The bed was redder than a butcher's counter."

"And who's suspected of the crime?" Mr. Burns enquired.

"The murderer's still on the loose, and most likely far away," said Monsieur Poder with a bitter smile. "They say the commissioner was on the trail of Petit-Radet."

"There's no end to what 'they say,' " said Monsieur de Pinville. "It looks to me like an act of revenge."

I couldn't help thinking that the commissioner had met his death in exactly the same way as Jean the Nightbird.

"I'm probably one of the last persons to have seen him alive," remarked my father. "He came to my shop yesterday, just before Mr. Burns paid us a visit. Do you remember, my friend?"

"Of course," said Mr. Burns, with a sad air. "He even asked you who I was."

"Father," I interrupted; "If you don't mind, I'm going to hear what they say around town."

He nodded and I went away. The voice of Mr. Burns, higher than the others, echoed in my ears.

"It's war, I tell you. Before a month goes by we'll hear the big guns."

Outside the streets were still crowded. I saw Nicolas coming along the Rue de Siam in the company of three young Navy Guards.

"Have you heard the news?" I called out.

"Good news, I call it, if that swine of a Duglois is dead. He'll have his little nest in hell."

The Navy Guards burst into loud laughter. Shrugging my shoulders I walked toward the penitentiary. On the way I met a bunch of ragamuffins from Kéravel, who were singing:

The top copper's dead
All the constables' eyes are red;
Nobody is safe in bed . . .

This, then, was Monsieur Duglois's funeral oration. I reflected again that Petit-Radet's enemies were doomed to be struck down, one by one.

15

At this point we were entering the month of August, which was to bring with it the climax of my story. Ever since I had let myself get involved in the affairs of Jean the Nightbird I had lost the carefree spirit natural to my age. The passage of time had obliterated the details of my first misadventure, but I was left with a feeling of melancholy and the premonition of some future disaster. I looked forward to the date of my entry into the artillery school. Once I had put on my new uniform I should be able to free myself of the past. In six weeks my father would reserve a place for me in the stagecoach to Landerneau, and from there I would travel to Rennes, Paris, Châlons, and Metz. The prospect of this journey occupied a large part of my imagination. Yes, I was too serious-minded for my age, and too given to daydreaming. Mr. Burns was quite right when he so wisely tried to curb my taste for adventure. My native ingenuousness made me an easy mark for any smooth-talking schemer.

"Don't let 'I'd never have believed it' serve you as an excuse," Mr. Burns told me. "You'll have to bear the marks that life will leave upon you. True friendship is a rare coin and one which few men are willing to part with. But you mustn't become a cynic. Love your fellow man, but keep your hand on the hilt of your sword until you're sure of him. Don't trust your first impulse until you have experience with which to back it."

I enjoyed, as I have said before, serious conversation, and Mr. Burns's good influence was due largely to the fact that he treated me not as an excitable schoolboy but as a full-grown man. Like Father Munien, he was a born teacher, but one whose worldly lore had endowed him with greater humanity.

But it is time to return to the mainstream of my story.

Mr. Burns continued to come to see us, although he often absented himself more than once in the same week and my father jokingly accused him of leading a double life. This invariably put Mr. Burns in a good humor. He adjusted the ruffle of his shirt and arched the calf of his leg as if he were about to do a sailor's jig.

Every morning I took him the *Gazette de France,* which he was supposed to bring back in the evening to my father. On the now frequent occasions when Madame Le Meur told me that he was away, I was at a loss as to what to do. I wandered disconsolately around the harbor, watching the convicts, who were at work in the hot sun.

One of these days—the seventh of August, if memory

155

does not deceive me—Madame Le Meur told me that Mr. Burns had left the house at dawn, saying that he would not be back until the following afternoon. After a listless "thank you" I went to kill the time before lunch on the docks. Nicolas had gone to Quimper, where he hoped to obtain from a rich uncle who had helped him in the past, the promise of a small monthly allowance that would enable him to study in Paris. It was agreed that we would travel as far as Paris together.

I was walking aimlessly along, musing on these things, when I found myself, quite unexpectedly, in the presence of the figurehead of the *Rose of Savannah,* the dusky girl who had so enflamed my imagination. Now she seemed to me much less glamorous, no longer a goddess of the tropical isles but simply a common female, carved out of wood eroded by the salt of the sea. Mr. Burns, I reflected, would be glad to know that I had come around to a less blindly romantic view.

I was surprised to see that the *Rose of Savannah* was tied up at the dock as informally as any other merchant ship of good standing. At the stern a sailor whom I had never seen before was sharpening a knife on a grinder which he worked with a footpedal. He wore an orange-and-blue silk scarf, like the one I remembered on the pock-marked lieutenant. Decidedly the *Rose of Savannah* had, like the Sleeping Beauty, emerged from her sleep, or rather from her captivity. The soldiers of the Karrer regiment, who had been watching over her, were all gone. No sign of the sentinel who, gun on shoulder, had paced the deck only a short time before.

"The *Rose of Savannah*'s no longer under guard?" I asked young Yannik, who was baiting his hook not far from the hull.

"You can see for yourself. The black lady has come out of the affair whiter than the ermine of our Breton flag!"

"How long has she been free?"

"Only since yesterday. For the last week I've been fishing here, and yesterday I saw the change of the guard for the last time. The *Rose of Savannah* has her papers in order. All she needs is a new owner."

"You must be joking."

"Nossiree! She's on the market, together with the services of her crew."

"Is the pock-marked lieutenant still aboard?"

"I don't know anyone with pock marks. I know the captain, though. He's a dark little fellow, always on the move, with a singsong voice that must come from south of the Loire."

Suddenly I had a wild idea. Why shouldn't Mr. Burns —who had the time, the means, and the experience— join together with my father to buy the *Rose of Savannah* and equip her for going to sea? The first thing would be to change her name to that of Mr. Burns's former ship, the *Mercy*. And why couldn't Burns and Morgat put the heraldic ermine of Brittany on their company flag? The idea was so intoxicating that the blood went to my head and I wanted to transform it into reality without delay. Of course it was too good to be true! Doubtless a dozen businessmen of the town had their eye on the ship and would push up the price if she went on the auction block. There was no time to lose, and what irked me most was that Mr. Burns should be away. Perhaps he had come back earlier than he said. I couldn't resist going to see, and took the ferry over to Recouvrance in order to find out more quickly. I ran like winged Mercury up the

157

rocky road, so fast, indeed, that I stumbled repeatedly and almost fell.

When I arrived at the house my heart sank, for Mr. Burns's shutters were still closed. Clinging stubbornly to my idea, I pushed open the gate and looked, in vain, for Madame Le Meur in the garden. My obstinacy was really extreme, for she had told me only a short time before that he would not return until the next day. And midday dinner was waiting for me at home. It would have been more reasonable to set forth my idea to my father and then to Mr. Burns. But I had a hunch that Mr. Burns would be more easily won over by my enthusiasm and more able, also, to persuade my father.

In this dilemma, I found myself involuntarily half-hidden by a privet hedge, when the garden gate swung open again, admitting a youthful female figure which was not that of Madame Le Meur. In spite of the heat the young woman was wearing the collar of her jacket turned up in such a way as to conceal her face. But what really made me start were her swinging gait and the click of her high heels on the pebbles. Who was it that walked just this way? No one but Manon! And the police had set a price on her lovely head!

With her face still concealed from me, she entered the house and shut the door behind her. I heard her go up the stairs and knock at another door, all too familiar to me. Breathlessly I waited to find out what was going to happen. If the door were to open I might not hear it, but if no one were there I should hear the click of her heels again on the stairs. I waited for almost a quarter of an hour. She did not come down and I could only conclude that Mr. Burns was in his room and had opened the door.

All the unsolved mysteries of the past months rose up

to haunt me. My head spun and I was deathly afraid, above all of being caught at what looked very much like willful spying. Gliding from bush to bush I managed to make my way inconspicuously to the garden gate. Once I was safely on the street tears welled up in my eyes and I had to clench my fists to contain my emotion. Needless to say, I was late for dinner.

"We've said the blessing," my father observed sternly.

I buried my nose in my plate and Marianne brought in my warmed-over meal.

"Where were you?" my father asked.

"At Mr. Burns's. But he wasn't there."

"That's no excuse for lateness. My son, I think the discipline of the school will do you good."

"Father," I said uneasily, "I'm not as careless as you think." And I told him about the absence of Madame Le Meur, the closed shutters, and the visit of the mysterious young woman whose silhouette seemed to me to be that of Manon de Gwened.

"A silhouette is not a certainty," said my father. "And you know you have a way of building things up in your imagination. There are dozens of girls like Manon, and I doubt that this one even looked like her. You say yourself that you didn't see her face. Yes, I believe that Metz is the place for you. Here at Brest there are too many dubious goings-on and too many unsavory people. Your ingenuousness allows you to be taken in and then to suffer. Three weeks from now you'll be in exciting new surroundings and the proud possessor of a cadet's uniform. I've already written to inform your uncle of your arrival. And before that you and Nicolas will have an interesting stagecoach journey."

I leaned over and grasped my father's arm.

160

"Father, I may be mistaken. I can't swear that the girl was Manon. But there are all sorts of loose ends to the story that I can't get out of my mind. Sometimes I think, like you, that its all the product of an overexcited imagination; other times I believe that a real danger threatens our friend Mr. Burns. I can't forget the murders of Jean the Nightbird and of Monsieur Duglois, both of them signed, so to speak, with the same knife. And the *Rose of Savannah* . . ." I stopped short, thinking of the object of my visit to Mr. Burns.

"How does the *Rose of Savannah* come into the story?" asked my father.

"For a whole week I thought that she belonged to Petit-Radet."

And at last I told him about my first sight of the pockmarked lieutenant and about the mysterious man with the troublingly familiar voice who had swept by me on the path to the Castle. My father listened attentively to my confession. He had gone to lean against the counter and stood there, his hands crossed behind his back, without interrupting me. When I had finished he rubbed his chin in the way that was always a sign of worry.

"Good boy, Yves-Marie. But you should have spoken to me sooner."

"I wasn't too sure what to think, Father, and I didn't want to give you any cause for alarm. Believe me, even in my adventure with Jean the Nightbird I never meant to do anything wrong. Even today I'm convinced that both he and Monsieur Duglois lost their lives because they knew some terrible secret. Yes, I believe that Petit-Radet is somewhere in Brest and that Mr. Burns's life is in danger."

My father tapped his well-shaven cheeks and nodded.

161

"You may be right, Yves-Marie. You'd better go over to Recouvrance again and see if he's there. Because he has no inkling . . . I've never seen him show the least sign of fear. He's a man hardened to danger, and pays no attention to it. But his very lack of suspicion may cost him dear."

"I'll tell him that by sheer chance I saw this young woman who looks so much like Manon . . ."

"Yes, you may as well say so. Her visit may have some bearing on the situation. He alone can know."

I put on my hat and went off to Recouvrance for the third time in the course of the day. I was so lost in thought that I bumped right into Madame Le Meur, who was just leaving the house.

"Young Monsieur Morgat, you're in a terrible hurry! You very nearly knocked me down! Well, your Mr. Burns is there. He came back sooner than he had expected. You can go on up."

With three leaps I was at the head of the stairs. I didn't have to knock at the door, for it opened to let me in. Mr. Burns stood there, smiling. "You're as red as a ship's lantern!" he exclaimed. "And blowing like a whale! Sit down, and we'll open a bottle of new cider."

"I came early this morning to bring you the *Gazette,* and Madame Le Meur said that you were away and wouldn't be back until tomorrow."

"That's what I told her to say. The truth of the matter is that I was expecting a caller and wished to be alone."

"Mr. Burns," I said, rising to my feet in order to control my emotion. "I have something else to tell you, and you must promise to believe me. It was by sheer accident that I saw something I perhaps shouldn't have seen. You see, I came to look for you again, around half past

162

eleven, and, as I say, by sheer accident I saw a young woman enter the house. I heard her climb the stairs . . . and then she didn't come down. And, although I couldn't see her face, she looked strangely like Manon, the girl from the 'Firebrand.' "

"By God, that's true!" said Mr. Burns, "although I'd never thought of it. She *does* have a way of walking like Manon's."

"It was all quite unintentional on my part, I assure you," I repeated. "I never meant to intrude on any secret."

"There, there, my boy! I believe you. Besides, you did nothing wrong. There's no secret, really. It's just that when a lady comes to see me I have to be discreet."

There was something not completely frank in his expression.

"You mean she's your mistress?"

"No, my romantic young friend, neither my mistress nor an unsuspected daughter. Simply a lady who doesn't wish to be known. And I must respect her desire. She has all sorts of troubles and sometimes she calls on me for advice."

He emptied the bottle of cider, and I gulped down my share. The dust of the road had left my throat dry. I chose to take comfort from Mr. Burns's explanation. And as my spirits lifted, I thought again of my great and glorious plan.

"Did you know, Mr. Burns, that the *Rose of Savannah* is no longer under watch?"

"What's that?"

"The soldiers have gone away. And she's a beauty of a ship, isn't she?"

I waited for a reaction, but Mr. Burns said nothing.

"I was thinking . . ." I went on, "and please don't laugh at my idea . . . that my father and you . . . you and my father . . . the two of you . . . might buy her. As her new owners you could change her name and call her the *Mercy*." Mr. Burns's blue eyes gleamed like those of a cat.

"Not a bad idea at all, my little artilleryman!"

He took his big tricorn hat and his cane in hand. "How do we get from here to where she's docked? We must find out, of course, whether she's really for sale."

"We'd have to change the figurehead."

"That's the least of the changes, my boy."

As we walked along Mr. Burns let me talk freely. But when we came to the dock where I had seen the *Rose of Savannah* earlier in the day I peered about me incredulously, and swore under my breath.

"What's the matter?" asked Mr. Burns, with a scrutinizing look.

"She's gone!"

"Well, well, well! The *Rose of Savannah* has slipped anchor. We'll have to make the best of it, that's all. For the present it's no use to think up a design for our company flag!" With that he twirled his cane and turned his back on the empty harbor.

164

16

And so the purchase of the enigmatic *Rose of Savannah* was put off until her improbable return, and I didn't even mention it to my father. As a matter of fact, I was none too sure that Mr. Burns had taken me seriously.

He and my father had a long talk together over their pipes, in the room at the back of the shop, where I thought it tactful to leave them alone. I knew that my father was trying to persuade his new friend to be more cautious and recalling to him the series of minor events that pointed to some sort of danger. I stood looking through the glass-paned front door, at the passers-by: the costumed peasant women on their way to the Seven Saints market and carters who were bringing up merchandise from the port. Every now and then Mr. Burns spoke loudly enough so that I could hear him.

"I'm most grateful for your warning. By George, you're opening my eyes and ears to things I never suspected. I didn't think I had an enemy in the world!"

My father insisted, and a few minutes later they came to the front of the shop. Mr. Burns examined a compass that my father had on display. He had a somewhat preoccupied air. After fingering a number of other objects, he emerged from his apparent daydreaming and said to my father. "I'm quite out of tobacco. I always let myself fall short this way. Could you get young Yannik to bring me a case of twenty-five packets? Then I'll have enough to last me for some time. No more empty jar, just when my pipe needs filling."

"That's easy enough," said my father. "I've just got in some good weed from Havana. It won't last long, because I already have an order to supply the officers of the *Néère*. By the way . . ." He turned toward me and continued. "Speaking of the *Néère*, I have good news for you, Yves-Marie. The tobacco is to be delivered at Ouessant, and I've made arrangements with Digwener to take it there in his *Rose-de-Marie*. He'll be ready at high tide, early tomorrow morning, and you can go along with him. You can spend the night with Kilvinec and pick up some orders for me and also for Monsieur Gouvat. I'll put it all down in writing, because I know that mathematicians are notoriously absentminded."

Mr. Burns smiled benevolently. "You have a fine day ahead of you. I only wish I could come along."

"Perfect, Mr. Burns! I take you at your word. It would be an enormous pleasure."

"Alas, Little Morgat, I spoke on sheer impulse. It so

happens that I may have to be away for the next few days. I must go again to defend the interests of an unfortunate woman before the court at Quimper."

This last phrase I didn't find too convincing. The young woman I had glimpsed in Madame Le Meur's garden didn't look the least bit unfortunate or unhappy to me. But I was too excited about the next day's trip to put my mind on Mr. Burns's affairs.

There was nohing I liked better than going out with one of the fishermen. I promised myself to come home with a basketful of skate and mullet and sole. We might even pick up a lobster pot, and I should get a lobster or one of the big, tasty crabs we called "sleepers."

"Hurrah!" I said, pushing open the kitchen door. "Marianne, will you put me up a picnic lunch? I'll take it away with me at the crack of dawn tomorrow. I'm going fishing."

Marianne shook her head and mumbled some indistinct words. She did not care at all for the sea; the mere mention of it made her think of the dead men who were said to still inhabit Ker-Is, the city swallowed up by the waves, and she never set foot on a boat without making the sign of the cross.

The sun had not yet risen when I arrived at the docks, my picnic basket under my arm, looking for the *Rose-de-Marie*. Finally I made out its somber outline. A sail was stretched out, like a tent, over the sleeping crew, a sailor known as Tintin, and a deck boy called Sylvestrick. Digwener had not yet arrived, and I sat down at the edge of the dock to wait for him. Although my father had sent a dozen bottles of cider aboard, along with the tobacco, for the purpose of making my presence agreeable to the crew, I didn't wish to wake them up too early. I was half-asleep myself when I was roused by the clatter of wooden shoes and saw the tall figure of Digwener with a basket on each arm.

"Little Morgat! You're not late, sailor, that's certain!"

I followed him up the gangplank, and our arrival awakened the crew. Sylvestrick, a stout fellow fifteen years old, was the first to pull himself to his feet, rubbing his eyes, and old Tintin did the same thing a moment later. Digwener distributed portions of rum, and I held out my cup and drank my share without batting an eyelash.

We rowed out of the Penfeld, waiting to pick up the wind. At the opportune moment Digwener and Sylvestrick raised the flapping mainsail while Tintin took the tiller and waited for the skipper to give the signal for tacking.

Now the boat scudded over the water like a sea gull skimming the waves in search of fish. We went past the *Danaë,* where fifes and drums were sounding reveille. On the port side the coast glided by. But fog still overhung the sun.

"We'll have rough going between Molène and Ouessant," said Digwener. "But by the grace of Saint Anne of Auray we'll be there by nightfall."

The wind was blowing from the stern and pushing us along. Digwener added a pole to the mast and a flying jib to the bowsprit. The cutter was using every inch of her canvas. I lay flat on my stomach at the bow, watching the water foam up at either side of the keel.

"You mustn't look too hard at the water," said Tintin. "The dead don't want you to meddle in their affairs. If they start making signs at you, you'll fall under their spell and be drawn down under the water."

"You can always protect yourself with the sign of the cross," said the deck boy.

"It doesn't always work," Tintin retorted.

"A sailor watches the clouds by day and the stars by night," Digwener put in. "We get our clues from the sky, not the sea."

"Well spoken," said Tintin.

"When Le Conquet is behind us we'll see no more than if we were looking straight into hell, if you'll allow me to say so," said the skipper.

"It was in weather like this that Le Maout heard the fatal horn . . ."

"That may be, but I doubt it. Our waters have been blessed, and so the "Flying Dutchman" doesn't come this way. More likely he heard the call of the wizard Merlin, who came from the mountains of Argoat. Water reflects sounds the way a mirror reflects images. Sylvestrick, the storm jib!"

"Yes, master, Lord help us! They say the men of Loguivy can see through the fog like the giant octopuses of the Indian Ocean."

"Anything's possible at sea. Sea and land are two quite different propositions. What goes on one doesn't go on the other. Tintin, you can prepare to change tack."

In the moment of silence that followed the deck boy began to sing:

The bells of Guiméné
And the big bell of Quimperlé
Ring out the wedding dance,
Gay, gay, gay!

"No singing when you can't see your way!" the skipper

shouted. "Do you hear, Sylvestrick? If you don't pipe down I'll find a way to stop you."

Digwener left Tintin at the tiller and came up to the bow.

"No seasickness, eh, Little Morgat? That means you're a real man." Turning his head slightly to the right he sniffed at the fog and stared into the gray sky.

"Blow the horn, Sylvestrick! Louder! We're at sea, you know! Le Conquet is astern, and by the grace of Saint Anne the fog will lift at noon. We can count on a fish-fry at Kilvinec's this evening."

"And what about lunch?" asked the deck boy.

"A sea hog, are you? Always an empty belly! We'll have lunch at noon, or whenever the sun breaks through . . . Meanwhile, blow your horn! Nobody can hear you."

Poor Sylvestrick almost burst his lungs in order to draw a mournful sound out of the horn. Soon we heard another horn answer from far away.

"Good grief!" Digwener exclaimed. "It's almost as crowded out here as on the Rue de Siam on a market day. Go to it, Sylvestrick, my boy!"

I clung to the deck, flat on my stomach, in order not to be knocked over by the boom as, with every change of tack, it swept across the deck. The fog lent the whole picture the aspect of a dream.

While Sylvestrick blew mournfully into his horn he cast side-glances at the sketchy lunch which Tintin was lining up on a barrel head: a loaf of black bread, some salt pork that smelled of fish and three bottles of cider. Digwener uncorked one of them and poured the contents into our tin cups. "To Saint Anne of Auray!"

He emptied his cup, refilled it, and raised it again.

"To the health of Monsieur Jean-Sébastien Morgat!" he said, looking me in the eye.

Silently we munched at our salt pork and bread. There was little reason for lingering at the "table." As we were draining our last cup of cider a feeble ray of light broke through the gray clouds.

"The sun!" exclaimed Tintin. "We'll be there by dark." Sylvestrick hung the horn on the cabin door and Digwener blew his nose into his hands.

"By Saint Anne, just listen to that!"

We pricked up our ears. From behind the clouds, which were now retreating like sheep toward the western horizon, there came a succession of detonations.

"Cannons, my boys!" Digwener exclaimed.

The noise was rolling toward us like a wagonload of rocks being dumped onto a highroad.

"The King's Navy attacking Petit-Radet, no doubt," I suggested. "They say that his ship was built in England."

Digwener leaned forward, bracing himself on the bowsprit, in an attempt to place the cannon fire more exactly.

"It's from between Molène and Ouessant, no doubt about it," he concluded.

"Then we shan't sleep at Kilvinec's tonight," said Tintin pessimistically.

Digwener had a perplexed air as, with his hands behind his back, he looked out over the greenish sea. The sun was shining brightly as it drove the clouds away. "Hard over to starboard!" he commanded. "We'll put in at Quéménez, where I've made soundings and holed up before. It's wiser to wait there for a while than to get ourselves into trouble."

I agreed. Already we were in sight of the green island of Quéménez, where a few hardy fishermen had plowed the land and planted vegetables. Their low-lying houses came into plain view, and at the western extremity of the island we saw two windblown women, staring out to sea.

"Shall we lower the rowboat?" asked Tintin.

"I should say not! Aren't you content to stay aboard? If time weighs on your hands, throw out a fishing line. An hour from now we'll be under sail again."

The island had no harbor, but we lowered the anchor some hundred yards offshore. The two women called out: "Ho, there, aboard the cutter? What do you know?"

Digwener took his megaphone and called back:

"Not a thing! Petit-Radet may be making trouble."

We saw the two women make the sign of the cross. The cannon shots were so loud that it seemed as if there must be a full-scale naval battle.

"The fellow's a fighter, if it's really he," Digwener admitted.

All of a sudden Sylvestrick shouted, "Portside, a sail, a sail! A frigate, that's what I call it."

Cautiously we let ourselves drift in the direction to which he was pointing. A frigate was indeed bearing down on us, driven by the wind, her sails flapping wildly.

"She's been hit," cried out Tintin.

The frigate seemed dangerously out of control. Listing heavily to one side she abruptly changed direction and moved back out to sea. Soon she was out of sight altogether. The cannonade had ceased, and only the shrill cries of gulls broke the silence of the sea.

"Sailor! Are you daydreaming? Hoist the mainsail and the storm jib! Little Morgat, you can lend him a hand."

I helped Tintin with the sails, while Sylvestrick turned the capstan and wound in the anchor. We set our course straight on Ouessant. Digwener held the tiller, a bearded

Neptune wearing a red wool cap, while Tintin and Sylvestrick kept watch for the barely visible rocks whose dangers they knew so well. In order to get through the Great Current we let ourselves be carried slightly to the south. In the distance the island of Ouessant looked like a purple cloud resting on the sea. All was calm and, strange to say, there were no traces of what had sounded like so violent a battle.

"The squadron must have put out to sea," said Digwener. "But I don't understand the movements of that solitary frigate. She looked badly enough damaged to run for shelter and repairs."

"Perhaps she's Petit-Radet's ship," Sylvestrick suggested.

"Nonsense, boy! Since when has a pirate taken over a royal frigate? It's quite bad enough if Petit-Radet has a schooner under his feet. Keep your eyes peeled, and if you see a schooner limping along with half her mainmast gone, then I'll grant you she belongs to Petit-Radet."

The island loomed up larger and larger before us.

"God and Saint Anne be praised!" Digwener exclaimed. "With their help we're through the Current."

We came into the harbor of Portz-Pol, where the whole population of some fifty souls, including the mayor, was waiting to greet us. Kilvinec stepped forward and waved to me, and I joyfully responded. The sea battle was on everyone's tongue; indeed, it was this that made for so much excitement over our arrival.

"You can thank God you're alive! Weren't you in the thick of it?"

"God save us! How did you get through?"

Standing up under a shower of questions, we realized that we had, quite unknowingly, had a narrow escape.

I went with Kilvinec straight to his house, leaving the errands with which my father had charged me until the morrow. Digwener and his crew came after, because Kilvinec let out beds and provided meals for the rare visitors to the island. The beds were in a loft over a stable, where he kept a phenomenally small cow and two dwarf sheep.

Along the way the islanders continued to press us with questions. They knew nothing of the battle; some thought that Petit-Radet and his schooner had been tracked down and sunk; others that the combattants were an English squadron, commanded by Admiral Keppel, and a French squadron, under Monsieur d'Orvilliers, which had put it to flight. A thick fog had covered the engagement, and only at the end had they seen two big ships sailing away toward the south.

"It's war," groaned the women.

And to the tune of this lament we arrived at Kilvinec's house. A dozen hens and a cock were scratching about in a pile of fish heads to one side of the door. The small crowd surged with us into the single large room, whose most valuable furnishings were a box bed and a carved oak wardrobe at the far end.

"I'm hungry," said Digwener, over the tumult.

Kilvinec, aided by Sylvestrick, fried the fish.

"I don't believe Petit-Radet was in the fight," said one of the fishermen. "He wouldn't have walked into the trap."

"I'm hungry," Digwener's booming voice repeated.

The clatter of plates and forks as they were laid out on the long table prevented us from hearing the door open. Suddenly we saw a man in a torn, dripping-wet uniform of the Royal Vessels regiment, who had apparently lost his cap, gun, and other accoutrements.

174

"Good people, I have news for you!" he announced. "Petit-Radet is finished. I fell into the water just when his ship was boarded, and I don't know how I happen to be alive to tell the tale."

A pool of water had formed around his feet and he was shaking all over. "I'm half-frozen, good people. Give me some hot cider."

Digwener caught him before he could fall.

"Poor fellow, he's at the end of his rope!" said a woman's voice.

17

The soldier required immediate care. Kilvinec lent him some clothes and we hung up his wet uniform in front of the fire. The poor fellow gaped at the preparations for supper and stared vacantly at the people around him. But a bowl of fish soup and a cup of hot cider went far toward bringing him around and soon he was able to tell us his name and his story. His name—or at least the only one he knew—was Periwinkle, he came from the Vermandois region and had served for three years in the Royal Vessels regiment.

"I've fought the Red Indians of the Great Lakes," he said, "but let me tell you, good people, that I never had such a close shave as just now out there in the water."

"What about Petit-Radet?" asked the island women. "Is he dead?"

"If he's alive I don't give him much longer to live."

"Has he been taken prisoner?" Digwener put in.

"At this hour he is probably in irons in the hold of the *Néère*."

"The slippery eel! And did he have more than one ship?"

Periwinkle stood up as best he could to this volley of questions. Now that he was warm and well fed he revealed himself as eminently good-humored.

"Let him talk without interruption," said Kilvinec. "He can't answer so many of you at once. Go ahead, Periwinkle, and tell us the whole story."

Periwinkle gulped down some brandy, wiped his mustache with the back of his hand, and started to talk in earnest.

"We've been on the alert since early in the month, good people. Our captain, Monsieur de Guillestre, told us that we were going after a certain Nicolas Trubet from Groix, known as Petit-Radet."

"I knew a Trubet once upon a time," Digwener broke in.

"Don't interrupt," said Kilvinec firmly. "Periwinkle, go on."

"Yes, good people, let me talk and I'll tell you everything I know, everything I saw with my own eyes. On the seventh of the month my company, under the command of Monsieur de Guillestre, requisitioned lodgings at Le Conquet. We stayed there until the beginning of this week, when we were picked up—a hundred and twenty of us and two drummers—by the *Néère*. She anchored a few hundred feet offshore and the good weather made it simple enough for us to go aboard. It was only yesterday that the fog descended upon us and very nearly allowed Petit-Radet to slip through the noose.

"We didn't stay long aboard the *Néère*. After sailing around Ouessant on the tenth, we were put off on the island of Molène, where we commandeered the fishing boats as they came in for the night. Our mission was to patrol the waters around the island, a dozen men to a boat. The guess was that Petit-Radet, with the frigate on his tail, would put out to sea to wait for the English fleet of Admiral Keppel. The boldness with which he circulated among the islands justified the suspicion that he was intriguing with the English and enjoyed their support. On the eleventh—yesterday—a squad of grenadiers from our regiment came to join us, aboard a coast-guard lugger. All last night we kept watch behind stacked guns. At dawn the grenadiers were ordered aboard the *Couronne des Anges*."

"Young Goulven's boat," said Digwener. "I know her well."

"That may be, my good fellow. Anyhow, our grenadiers went off with a good number of grenades in their pouches and Monsieur de Guillestre himself to command them. We were left ashore, ready to sally forth in our boats whenever Monsieur Bourdin, our lieutenant of long standing, gave us the order.

"This morning, just before dawn, we heard cannon fire. Monsieur Bourdin ordered us to arm ourselves and stand by. The fog was so thick that a man couldn't see his own feet. The fishermen who owned the boats said it would be crazy to go to sea off this rocky coast in this weather.

" 'I don't give a tinker's dam for the rocks and the

179

weather,' said our lieutenant. 'Orders are orders, and I'm ready to look for Petit-Radet in the jaws of hell.'

"He knew how to talk. Beyond the fog we heard the cannon fire intensify. And the sound of a foghorn."

"That was me," said Sylvestrick.

"Shut up, you little dogfish!" Digwener shouted. "Leave the floor to your elders. You'd think the boy had caught Petit-Radet himself, single-handed!"

"Around seven o'clock," the soldier continued, "Monsieur Bourdin ordered us abroad the boats. We navigated like blind men, groping in the direction of the battle. The owner of my boat was a certain Bihan, a fellow as old as Methuselah, who knows the coast the way a miser knows his pocket. His beady, crablike eyes seemed to pierce the fog, and the rest of us could only commend our souls to the Lord and trust in his judgment. At ten o'clock in the morning there was a sudden silence, which froze us with fear. All of us realized that the fog was working on the pirate's behalf. Monsieur Bourdin sat with lowered head at the stern. He too must have thought that the fish had slipped through the net.

"At noon the fog suddenly parted, revealing the sun. The sea around us was crowded with craft of every description. In the distance two frigates and a lugger were tracing circles. One of the frigates bore marks of battle; she listed to one side and moved as jerkily as a wagon on a rocky mountain road. The water was filled with debris. 'There's a piece of a schooner,' said old Bihan.

"Just then one of the frigates shifted direction and set her course directly on an island, probably this one. 'She's sighted the prey,' said Bihan, 'and she's giving chase.' A moment later our deck-boy shouted, 'Starboard! Jesus save us! Starboard!'

"Bearing down on us was a schooner as pretty as any you could hope to see, whose figurehead was the bust of a black girl from some savage island. Bihan threw the tiller over, and we glided by. 'Fire!' shouted Monsieur Bourdin.

"Our guns were ready, and we let loose a volley. The air was filled with smoke and the sharp smell of gunpowder pricked our nostrils. Meanwhile there was a series of clicks as we jammed the ramrods into the gun barrels and reloaded. When the smoke had blown away we saw the schooner a couple of hundred yards ahead of us. A powerfully built man was aiming an eight-pounder, set in a gunport, in our direction. We saw him light the fuse, but before we could change our course the cannon ball struck down our mast. A yard rope looped itself around me and carried me overboard. I sank into the water as heavily as if there were lead in my breeches. When I came to the surface I managed to catch hold of a floating bowsprit. I pulled myself up and straddled it, thanking God for having brought me to relative safety. After I had rubbed the salt water out of my eyes I looked around me. And what a sight met my eyes! The *Couronne des Anges* had caught up with the pirate schooner and our twenty grenadiers, led by Monsieur de Guillestre, had hooked her with grappling irons. After a volley of grenades they boarded her on the starboard side. The hulking fellow who had aimed the cannon at our craft and scattered our little crew over the blood-stained water defended himself like a lion. I could hear the hoarse cry he emitted every time he brought a gun barrel down on one of our lads' heads. Finally Monsieur de Guillestre ran a sword through one of his legs and he collapsed on the deck. Our fellows lost no time in tying him to the carriage of the eight-pounder. I waved and shouted in an attempt to catch their attention, but in vain. Some of my companions, who were closer than I, did make themselves heard and a few minutes later they were climbing up ropes onto the deck of the schooner.

"The two ships, still grappled together, began drifting toward the coast, leaving me astride my improvised raft. I had got rid of my shoulder belt, knapsack, and cartridge pouch, and the bowsprit was quite strong enough to support me. I paddled with my hands, resting at intervals, flat on my stomach. For five hours I progressed in this fashion, and if it hadn't been for a favorable current I'm not sure I would have landed on this rocky shore alive. I owe a candle, at the very least, to Our Lady. Finally a wave did roll me onto your doorstep, and I'm grateful for the aid and comfort you've given me. In return I have brought you a piece of good news. From now on you can put to sea without fear. I trust that Nicolas Trubet, known as Petit-Radet, is on his way to prison, and that his companions will share the same fate, if they haven't been killed. I propose a toast to the grenadiers of the Royal Vessels regiment, our deliverers!"

He raised his cup of cider and drank it down, clicking his tongue with relish.

"Soldier," said Kilvinec, "if your story is true, it's the best news of the last half century. Drink up, and eat your fill of fish and salt pork. You can thank God for your good fortune."

I had remained silent while the soldier told his story. But when he described the figurehead of what was unquestionably the *Rose of Savannah* my blood curdled. All the events of the past winter and spring whirled about in my head. The *Rose of Savannah* was, indeed, Petit-Radet's ship, and he had had the unspeakable boldness to anchor her in the citadel of his enemies! There was no doubt, now, in my mind that he was the pock-marked individual who had received me on board and even come to the shop to bring me a message. I would have given anything for a pair of wings with which to fly to Brest and see the fellow with my own eyes before he was taken to Rennes for trial. I didn't know, of course, that a special court-martial was to be set up at Brest to judge him and his seven surviving companions.

Meanwhile I thought it best to hold my tongue and listen to what the others were saying. The long day at sea had left me sleepy and I was stiff "from the keel to the top of the mainmast," as Digwener used to say when he had a fever.

"I still don't understand the layout of the battle," said Kilvinec. "All we saw from here was a frigate, apparently damaged and drifting with the wind. We were all looking toward the west at the time, because we thought the frigate was English."

"This is the story," the soldier told him. "The bulk of the action took place to the east, between Ouessant and Molène, and within half an hour it was over. The trap was laid there, and there it was sprung. The pirate fought like a lion, adding more items to the list of murders with which the judges will charge him."

"They'll be hanged, the lot of them," said Digwener, "and I intend to be there, cost what it may, yes, even if I have to lose a week's catch in the Bay of Biscay."

Just then the parish priest came into the room, following, as it were, the majority of his parishioners. A stalwart fellow he was, as I had had the occasion to know, always ready to help hoist a storm jib or haul a net when a fishing boat was shorthanded.

"Five more soldiers—four of them from the regiment of Brest—have swum ashore and are holed up at the rectory. They too were catapulted into the ocean during the battle. Rose Harlé, I want you to find them some dry clothes, and you, Kilvinec, to take them a pint of spirits. By tomorrow, God willing, they'll be able to rejoin their comrades in Brest. Harlé, you must make a special voyage to the mainland, and I'll go with you in order to give an account of what we saw, from this vantage point, of the events of such a momentous day."

He turned to Periwinkle and asked him a few questions, to which the soldier replied with an abridged version of his story.

"So you're quite sure that Petit-Radet is a prisoner, are you? The fifth of the escapees at the rectory belongs to *Néère*. The *Gracieuse,* he tells me, is the frigate which the *Rose of Savannah* took by surprise in the fog, crippled and put to rout. I'm happy to hear that your regiment effected the capture of these ruffians."

The priest had a word of greeting for everyone present and drank down a cup of cider. When his eyes fell on me, he exclaimed, "Little Morgat, aren't you?"

He remembered me, of course, from my father's shop, to which he paid frequent visits.

"You don't look like your usual self, my boy," he added. "Are you under the weather?" With that he picked up my hand and felt my pulse. "I don't like it, not at all. Obviously you have a fever. You must get a good night's rest, and I'll look in on you tomorrow."

184

I protested that I wasn't in the least ill, but even as I said these words I shivered all over.

"The boy's shaky as a leaf," said Rose Harlé, who was waiting to go with the priest to the rectory.

"Put him to bed," the priest insisted. "Wrap hot, wet towels around his feet and don't give him any supper. I'm worried by the fact that his hands are cold and clammy."

Kilvinec took me by the arm and installed me on the box bed, drawing the curtains so that I could undress in privacy. Once I was between the sheets my head felt incredibly heavy, and my thoughts scattered like sheep dispersed by a clap of thunder. Outside the curtains there was a murmur of compassionate voices, that of the priest the most distinct among them.

"It could be typhus," he was saying, "if it isn't the result of overexcitement."

My brain whirled, and a host of images rose up, as if in a nightmare, to assail me. My father, Petit-Radet, Mr. Burns, Kilvinec, Jean the Nightbird, and the lieutenant of the *Rose of Savannah*—Manon de Gwened, riding a broomstick, led the infernal dance.

18

For ten days I was semiconscious. It wasn't until nearly the end of August that I recovered my memory and became aware of what was going on around me.

At this point my father told me that I had been laid low by fever in the house of Kilvinec at Portz-Pol on the island of Ouessant and that the Abbé Duvard was the first to see how seriously I was affected. I remembered vaguely that, after listening to the story of the shipwrecked soldier, I had been put to bed. The next day, I now learned from my father, I was taken, along with the group of escapees from the battle, aboard the *Marie-de-France*. And once more the Abbé Duvard was my protector. The voyage was very nearly disastrous. Off the

Balannec Islands, just after we had crossed the Great Current, we ran into a heavy storm, in which we nearly lost our lives. By a miracle, Jean Harlé brought us through, and put us off at Le Conquet. The Abbé Duvard stayed with me all the way to Brest and "The Anchor of Mercy."

Father Antonelli, the director of the Hospital of the Brothers of Charity, which was a navy hospital as well, took me under his care. But of this period I remember nothing. The first face I recognized was that of my father, who was sitting beside my bed. And the next that of Marianne, when she brought me a bowl of steaming broth, which lit a gleam in my lackluster eyes.

"That's a boy!" exclaimed my father.

And Father Antonelli, when he paid his daily visit, said optimistically, "He's over the hump! Give him plenty to eat, but in small quantities and at frequent intervals. He's still as frail as a winter chick." And, tapping my cheek, the good Father added, "In a few weeks you'll put on your cadet's uniform, and that will be the last step of your cure. Meanwhile . . ." and he turned to my father ". . . no excitement."

"When can I get up and go out?" I said, barely trusting my own voice.

"Easy there, my boy! Before you can get out into the sun you must give proof of the common sense and self-discipline required of a future officer of the King's Artillery."

From this day on I made rapid improvement. Little by little I entered the blissful state known as convalescence. Marianne's good cooking built up my strength, even if I was still confined to bed. My father read aloud in order to give me some distraction, and in this way I became acquainted with Montesquieu's *Lettres persanes* and *L'esprit des lois*. Nicolas de Bricheny, Kilvinec, Digwener, Monsieur de Pinville, Goas, and Pillawer all came to see me, and the last-named brought me pears and apples from the inland markets he visited on his travels.

Of course, as I recovered my faculties I began to want to know what was going on. I bombarded my father with questions about the fate of Petit-Radet and his companions. And I was concerned about the prolonged absence of Mr. Burns. He had gone to Quimper, my father told me, and knew nothing of what had happened to me. But no doubt he would be back soon.

I stood looking out of the open window while Marianne made my bed. In spite of the fact that it was August I wore a winter dressing gown. How agreeable I found the scene below! I knew now the value of those trifles which, when added together, make up the enjoyment of life. The sea air swept into my lungs and revived my spirits. I heard drumbeats from the docks and thought to myself: "Another one of the king's regiments off to Canada!" I could recognize the drums of the Swiss and the fifes of the regiment of Brest as they played the old Norman march *Joli Tambour,* and *The Boys in Gray,* the march of the regiment of Champagne. All night long these tunes rang in my head, and I tossed on my pillow until I finally fell asleep.

My father had corroborated the details of the soldier's story of the capture of Petit-Radet. The town council of Brest had given a party in honor of his captors, the grenadiers of the Royal Vessels regiment. I was anxious, of course, to hear every particular. Confinement to my room, which I realized was necessary in my still weakened condition, had thrown me into a state of melancholy which none of my books had the power to dispel. My chief distraction was the daily visit of Nicolas who, incidentally, had persuaded his uncle to subsidize his stay in Paris. Every day I questioned him.

"Tell me, Nicolas, is there no news of Mr. Jerome Burns? If my calculations are correct it's three weeks that he's been gone. You might go find out if Madame Le Meur has any news of him."

"I've told you before that she has none. Burns never was one to talk much about his own affairs. Personally, I think he'll come back soon, out of curiosity about the trial of the pirates."

"Then he might go straight to Rennes?"

"To Rennes? Why to Rennes? But perhaps you don't know that a court-martial has been set up right here. Petit-Radet and his seven accomplices will be tried and hanged in Brest. Yesterday the *Rose of Savannah* was towed into port, by boats with convicts at the oars and crewmen of the *Néère* to keep the strokes in time with their whistles. Quite a sight, I can tell you! The ragged population of Kéravel was lined up on the shore, held back by the coppers. The whole mob—women and children included—had drunk so much spirits that it was completely out of hand. The soldiers of the Karrer regiment had to be called in to restore order, which they did by laying about the crowd with the butts of their rifles."

"And you saw the *Rose of Savannah* with your own eyes?"

"That I did, and in a sad state, without either masts or rigging! The deck is like a junk yard, with the cannons lying on their barrels and the carriages sticking up into the air like overturned giant turtles. The black girl at

189

the prow was the first to get her comeuppance; she had her head lopped off by a cannonball from the *Néère*. When the *Rose of Savannah* entered the river all the king's men aboard tossed their caps into the air. Laculas of the *Néère* was in command."

"And was Petit-Radet aboard too?"

"No. He and his companions, in irons, of course, were brought in on the *Néère* and transferred, under cover of darkness and the guard of a company of the regiment of Brest, to the underground cells of the Castle. At present their trial is in the process of preparation. It's generally thought that they'll be judged in a hurry, because war is at hand. The fleet is ready to sail, and the Duke of Chartres may sail with it, under the command of Monsieur d'Orvilliers."

"And Petit-Radet—what does he look like? Isn't he the big, pock-marked fellow I met on the *Rose of Savannah*?"

"I haven't seen him, myself. Nobody has, for that matter, except the grenadiers who captured him, the sailors who brought him in and, of course, the prison guards. But our curiosity will be satisfied soon enough, since he's to be hanged before the end of the month."

Nicolas was my best source of information. And according to him war was the main thing on everyone's mind. Now that Petit-Radet had been captured and was almost certainly slated for execution, there was no more reason to worry about him. People were worrying and talking, rather, about the war.

Perhaps because I was still confined to the house I continued to brood over the still unexplained happenings in which I had played a part. A dozen times a day I badgered my father about Mr. Burns and Petit-Radet.

190

"Will you go to the hanging?" I asked him.

"Indeed I won't. That's no pastime for a self-respecting man. Society has a right to rid itself of its enemies, but it's a vulgar sport to go to a killing."

"Father, if you knew how bored I am with being cooped up . . ."

"I understand, my boy. You'll have to be patient."

"But when, *when* can I go out?"

"As soon as the doctor says you're ready. Beginning today, after lunch, you can sit at the open window, and the sea air will serve as a tonic. You'll be well before you know it."

And so, wrapped up in a way quite unsuitable to the season, I spent my afternoons looking down at the Rue de Siam and the short span of the docks which was visible from my window. Not only did the color return to my cheeks, but my spirits revived as well. The familiar animation of the street seemed to me something new and wonderful, and I feasted my starving eyes upon it. On Friday—which was market day—there was a dazzling array of colors. The picturesque costumes of all the surrounding villages were represented. The women of Ploaré, for instance, were as richly dressed as the statues of saints carried in a procession. The variety of the embroidery on their bodices was a source of unending delight. Occasionally a "Léonarde" passed by, with a scarf that hung all the way to the ground, or a woman of the "Bigoud" region, with a cap shaped like a mitre and the embroidery of her bodice all orange and gold. From a distance I could see the sky-blue *chupens* or waistcoats of the men of the "Glazik" country, their pleated shirts and knee-high wool gaiters. Add to this gay peasant dress the uniforms of the regiments of Brest, the Royal

Marine, and the Royal Vessels, and you can form some idea of the spectacle before me. And then there were the king's sailors, the cadets of the Brest Naval Academy and the Flag Guards with their red stockings and their tricorn hats worn tilted to one side. Sometimes, in this motley crowd, I saw the face of someone I knew; I thrust my arm out the window and waved to him to come up and pay me a visit. This Friday, as I sat at my window as in a theater box, I caught sight of young Yannik. He was wearing what was obviously a new suit and twirling a sling around his head.

"Hello there, Yannik!" I called out.

He raised his head, saw me, and smiled broadly.

"Come on up!"

A moment later I heard him push open the door of "The Anchor of Mercy." The awkward but good-natured Yannik was a mine of information. Every bit of gossip between Kéravel and the Seven Saints was sure to find its way to his big ears.

"How handsome you are today!" I said, motioning to him to turn around so I could admire his new suit from every angle.

"My three sisters, my four brothers, and I have all got new clothes," he said proudly. "My father's been commissioned to build the gallows for the hangings. That's what we get for being neighbors to Cotentin Fiburce!"

Cotentin Fiburce was the hangman, whose house in Kéravel I described earlier. Like everyone else in the town, I knew him well. He was a tall, powerfully built fellow with courteous, self-effacing ways and resigned to being a man set apart and condemned to solitude. In his spare time he wove baskets; his two sons worked for local

193

butchers and his daughter wanted to become a nun.

"What do they say in Kéravel about the hanging?" I enquired.

"They're looking forward to the fun. There'll be eight ropes suspended from one big beam; just think of that, Little Morgat! My father designed it himself and the judges gave their approval. It will cost the town good money, and my father's received an advance already. That's the reason for my fine clothes. Every one of my sisters has a new dress and an embroidered apron."

"Has your father seen Petit-Radet?"

"Nobody's seen him. He was brought into town by night, like the king of the rats. The jailkeeper's son tells me he's a big fellow, with red hair, like mine, and a red beard. He has terrifying eyes, and he barked like a fox when he asked for water."

Two hours later a boy came to deliver a book from Monsieur Dacé's bookshop. He too knew the jailkeeper's son but, according to what he had been told Petit-Radet was short and stocky, with kinky black hair like that of an African and the cruel, protruding eyes of a giant octopus.

Marianne's friend, Rose Néré the laundress, maintained, on the other hand, that Petit-Radet was slim and trim, a Parisian pickpocket type, not the least impressive. It was difficult to choose among such varied descriptions. And none of them included the pock marks which would have enabled me to identify Petit-Radet as the unforgettable lieutenant of the *Rose of Savannah*. (I learned later that this fellow, whose name was Pedro de Luarca, had been killed by a grenade when the pirate ship was boarded off the Balannec Islands.)

194

Whenever he was not too busy in the shop, my father came to see me, usually bringing with him a book or some other small present.

"Here's something to take with you to the artillery school," he would say, sitting down beside me with a kind but melancholy smile, which never failed to touch my heart.

"Father, I'd give anything to see Mr. Burns. I have a feeling something has really happened to him. He's never been away this long before."

"It's not the first time, however, that he's left us without news . . ."

"Perhaps he'll never come back, then."

"Anything is possible," said my father. "We mustn't try to fathom the secrets of Divine Providence."

"True, Father. Old sea dogs, as you know better than I, are like gulls. They may alight and rest for a while after a long voyage, but no one can tame them and persuade them to stay."

"I'll tell Marianne to bring you a cup of hot chocolate. That will fix you up. In about an hour Pillawer's coming, bringing you a toilet case and a set of razors with blades of good Sheffield steel. You'll be the envy of all the other cadets at the artillery school."

My father smiled as he said these words, but I could see that there was something on his mind. He went over to the shelves where I kept Jean the Nightbird's statuettes and picked up the figure of a sailor leaning against a grappling iron. Before putting it back he gave a deep sigh.

"Exactly like the real thing, isn't it, Father?"

"God's designs are impenetrable," he said, with no apparent reference to my question.

As he went away I noticed that his shoulders were stooped, in a way that was not at all like him. And his footsteps echoed heavily on the stairs. Just before I went to bed Pillawer arrived, as my father had told me. When the toilet case was spread out on my bed I let out a cry of joy. There were bottles of cologne, a comb, scissors, and a case with two razors and a shaving brush. The case itself was of green leather with my initials engraved in gold upon it.

"Little Morgat, you can see how much your father loves you," said Pillawer. "I picked this case up at Quimper, where they had ordered it straight from the Palais Royal of Paris. The name is on the satin lining."

"What's happened to the trial of Petit-Radet?"

"It's scheduled for tomorrow. And it won't last long. The facts are there, and there's no possible defense against them."

"Are you going to the Esplanade on the day of the hanging?"

"Indeed I'm not. That's no sight for Christian eyes. 'An eye for an eye and a tooth for a tooth.' Let's not talk about it. By the way, you must make me a list of all the things you need to take with you. Your father just told me to buy them on his behalf. Next week I'm going to Rennes, where there's plenty of choice and good prices."

"Have you heard anything about Mr. Jerome Burns?"

"No, I haven't. What a man! You can never put your finger upon him."

"Has he kept the room at the house of Madame Le Meur?"

"I believe so, but I can't swear to it."

"Look here, could you try to find out when he'll be back? I'd be so happy to know . . ."

"I'll do what I can, but I doubt if the good lady knows any more than we do."

"I have a feeling there's bad luck in the air, Pillawer. My father's sad in a way that isn't like him. It wouldn't surprise me to hear that Mr. Burns is dead."

"Don't say such a thing, Little Morgat! Take another look at your toilet case, and dream of the sword you'll soon wear. That's better than brooding."

"Will you tell me about the trial?"

"Of course, Little Morgat. If I have anything to tell. Because, to be honest with you, the trial doesn't interest me—no, not at all."

19

A few days after Pillawer's visit I began to feel much better. My legs were no longer shaky and I had no more dizzy spells. I went downstairs and ate my meals with my father and Marianne in the back room of the shop, which was the coolest spot in the house. These were the hottest days of the year and indeed some of the hottest that Brest had ever known. At certain hours the air was positively suffocating and you could have fried an egg on the paving stones of the street outside. This was how I imagined the heat of Caracas, as Mr. Burns had so often described it.

I was not allowed to set foot on the street. At moments it occurred to me that this veto was not for reasons of health alone. My father's excessive severity must have had another motive, one I could not understand. When the sun was not too strong I stood at the open door and breathed deeply of the sea air. Occasionally I looked up at the new sign Nicolas had painted for us, but whose real inspiration had been Mr. Burns. I hoped my father was right in being so optimistic about his return. In my mind the unusual length of his absence was obscurely connected with the mysterious young woman I had glimpsed from Madame Le Meur's garden. But surely one day he would walk in the door and lean over the counter in the familiar way, to ask for his Puerto Rico tobacco.

At the table I talked repeatedly about his eloquence, erudition, and good humor. My father nodded, without making any reply, and changed the subject. Most often he spoke of my departure for Metz, which was only three weeks away. The imminence of this event distracted me from my worry about the prolonged absence of Mr. Burns, and the prospect of putting on the king's uniform erased, at times, my nostalgia for the little house at Recouvrance. But the memory of my visits there was indelibly printed on my mind. I could still see Mr. Burns emerge from behind the curtains, his long white clay pipe with the red tip in one hand.

One evening, just as we were getting up from the table, Pillawer dropped in. Under his arm he had a roll of paper which he unfolded on the counter.

"A picture of Nicolas Trubet, alias Petit-Radet," he exclaimed. "Not much to look at, but it should satisfy your curiosity."

The picture was a cheap print of the kind sold at country fairs, showing Nicolas Trubet as a bearded man with a ferocious look in his eye and a red kerchief with yellow flowers wound like a turban around his head. In his right hand was a sabre with a basket hilt and in the left a lighted fuse. Pistols and an exotic dagger were stuck into a green scarf which he wore around his waist. Such, then, in the artist's extravagant imagination, was the pirate who had made Neptune tremble and now, in all likelihood, would end his days on the gallows. The trial was already under way, and the clerk of the court, Monsieur Antoine Golomer, who bought tobacco at "The Anchor of Mercy" told us that the attitude of "Captain" Nicolas Trubet and his seven gentlemen of fortune was more cynical than anyone could have foreseen. The captain had categorically refused the services of a defense lawyer.

It was after one of the clerk's visits that my father told Marianne to lay out his best clothes for the next morning because he had to go, with Pillawer, to testify at the trial. This was startling news. What could my father have to say about Petit-Radet? Then I remembered the pock-marked lieutenant of the *Rose of Savannah* and the day that he had come to buy a lantern from us. Once more he was the center of my suspicions, for I did not know, at this point, that he was dead.

On Monday morning my father put on his fine brown wool suit, his silver-buckled shoes and his new, lace-trimmed hat. As he left the house he gave strict orders to the effect that I must stay home. I did not protest, because I was expecting a visit from Father Antonelli.

Nevertheless the day dragged by slowly. I wandered about my room, stood at the window, and sat down at my desk to look over the list of the first-year courses at the artillery school, of which Father Munien had managed to obtain a copy. My father came back, bringing Pillawer with him, at about six o'clock. I rushed down to meet them, and as I opened the door at the foot of the stairs I heard the name of Madame Le Meur. At once they changed the subject. My father's face was pale and drawn. He reached for the bottle of rum which he kept under the counter and asked Marianne to bring him two pewter goblets. At the same time he enquired after my health and behavior. Because I was vexed by his excessive concern I answered for her.

"I'm not dead, you can see that! In fact, I feel very well. I doubt that my health will get this much attention when I'm with my battery in the field."

"Our young cock has a red crest," said Pillawer, laughing. "It's obvious that he's ready to stretch his legs."

"I'm waiting for the doctor's orders," said my father.

"Then, Father, I can tell you something new. At the end of the week I am free to go where I please. Father Antonelli was here this afternoon and gave me permission. On Saturday afternoon I can go for a stroll."

"Did Father Antonelli prescribe a dose of rum to top off your cure?" asked my father, affectionately rumpling my hair.

"I only wish he had!"

My father clinked his goblet against that of Pillawer and drank deeply. Pillawer did not linger. He too seemed unhappy. As he went away he shook my hand with unusual emphasis, started to say something, then thought better of it and merely shrugged his shoulders.

"How was your day in court?" I asked my father. "Was your testimony useful? What does Petit-Radet, or Trubet, since that's his name, really look like?"

I asked these three questions almost brutally, to show that I was tired of being overprotected and left in ignorance of the events of the day. In a manner that was melancholy rather than ill-humored my father made a conscientious reply. The day had been tedious, he said, taken up with a mass of useless details, since the pirates' guilt was a foregone conclusion. His testimony had been relative to the police commissioner, who had been murdered shortly after his visit to our shop. Trubet had confessed to this murder as well as to that of Jean the Nightbird. When the judge asked him what were the motives of these two crimes he had answered: "One of them carried a statuette of me in his pocket and the other was entirely too curious about me. If I wanted to go on living they had to die. Yes, I killed the artist from the 'Big School' on the streets of Kéravel and your prying policeman in his bed. You may as well credit me with both crimes, although I have only one neck for the noose."

"Did you recognize Petit-Radet as someone you had seen before, Father?"

My father hesitated imperceptibly before lowering his eyes and saying firmly. "No, I didn't." And he added hastily, "Nicolas Trubet is to be hanged early in the morning of the day after tomorrow. Perhaps Father Antonelli will let you go out earlier than Saturday. We shall see." He swallowed his saliva as if every word had cost him an effort.

For the moment I could make no reply. Conflicting ideas danced in my head, and my father's cryptic manner only increased the feeling of uneasiness I had harbored during the last few days. But I did all I could to conceal my fears. That evening we spoke no more of Trubet and his band. I masked my anxiety by changing the subject to the artillery school.

"I stopped in at the post office on my way to court," said my father. "And, as I meant to tell you when I first came home, there was a letter from your uncle. He's looking forward to seeing you and will do everything in his power to make things agreeable. You'll be able to spend your Sundays at his house. And your cousin Estelle, it seems, is a young person of great charm and many qualities."

"I'm not exactly ready to set up housekeeping!" I said laughing.

"I should hope not! An officer shouldn't marry until he has rheumatism."

"What's that, Master?" said Marianne, with a scandalized air.

"Oh, are you there, Marianne? Give us a bottle of good Burgundy while we're waiting for our future lieutenant to find himself a wife."

Night brought me certainty, of a kind. I made up my mind to be present, cost what it might, at the execution of Petit-Radet and his companions.

The next day seemed interminable. As I stood at the door of "The Anchor of Mercy," brooding over my plan and waiting for time to drag slowly by, I heard the creak of wagon wheels going down the Rue de Siam in the direction of the docks. Astride one of the shafts sat Cotentin Fiburce, the hangman. One of his two sons was leading the horse while the other walked behind, carrying a sledgehammer on his shoulder. After them came Maheu the carpenter and my young friend, Yannik, who were trying to look more discreet about where they were going. I waved to Yannik and he dropped out of the little group and came over to the door. In reply to my questions he told me that they were on their way to set up the scaffold on the Esplanade, in front of the Castle.

"If you want to see tomorrow's show," he said, "I'll wait for you at five o'clock in the morning where the Rue de Siam meets the docks. Petit-Radet and his men will be turned over to Master Fiburce at about eight o'clock. I'll take you to a place where we'll have a box-seat view."

"Good!" I said. "I'll be there. But don't tell anyone. If my father finds out he'll stand guard at my door, halberd in hand."

"I'm no such fool. My father doesn't know what I'm up to, either. You have no idea of the excitement there is in the town. All the inns are full, and carriages and coaches are pouring in from Landerneau, Quimperlé, and Quimper. Other curiosity seekers are arriving by boat from Roscoff and Lorient. Rooms are going for astronomical prices. Kéravel, as you can imagine, is in a state of complete confusion. Thieves and pickpockets are leaguing together to rob the visitors. They say a cordon of troops will surround the whole section, beginning this evening. At the corner of the docks, in front of the penitentiary, a company of the Royal Vessels regiment is cooking soup behind stacked guns. We saw the men just now, as we passed by."

"I'll see you tomorrow then, Yannik."

"At five o'clock sharp, Little Morgat."

Yannik ran to catch up with his father. He had no sooner turned the corner than marching footsteps caught my attention. A company of the regiment of Brest, led by Captain Rateau, pike in hand, was coming down the street. I saluted the captain, whom I knew slightly, and he answered with a friendly wave of his left hand.

All day long an endless procession of constables,

mounted police, and soldiers filed by. Toward evening two squadrons of the Royal Cavalry, which were said to have been sent from Paramé, entered the town. Gossip traveled from one door to another, and children filled the streets, threading their way among the horses and adding to the festive confusion. My father was anything but happy with the sight.

"It's enough to make a man despair of the human race," he said. "I only wish Monsieur Jean-Jacques Rousseau were here to see. Philosophy can't stand up against folly."

Because of this disgust he closed the shop early and went to bed soon after supper. I too went up to my room, where the open window let in the cool night air. There was still noise below; little groups of people were talking in front of every door. But the noise subsided as patrols began to make their rounds and clear the streets.

I knew that I couldn't possibly sleep. I tried to read a book, but ghostly faces rose up between the lines. The next day would bring with it an end to my adventures and also their explanation. I wanted to know what it was all about, and to know from what I could see with my own eyes, to use a phrase that Mr. Jerome Burns had taught me. My resolution was hardened by the desire for certainty. My father might, indeed, be on the alert all night and even stand guard at the door, but I would not let him stop me. I heard the clock strike every hour of the night, followed by the singsong call, which seemed to me to have a truly funereal tone, of the night watchman. When dawn came it was dirty around the edges; the summer day was somehow spoiled before it had even begun. I plunged my head into a basin of cold water and got myself ready to go. It didn't take long, for impatience spurred my every gesture. I wished that some good fairy would pick me up and crary me to the place where my torment would come to an end and I should find peace and liberation. Before closing the window I looked up and down the street below. Everything was quiet, and the shutters were closed as far as I could see in either direction. I tiptoed down the stairs, holding my shoes in my hand, crossed the courtyard, and came to the storage shed and the back door. I paused to put on my shoes and started to walk out. Outside the door, not at all to my surprise, my father was waiting. I spoke up boldly.

"I have to go out, Father . . ." And when he failed to answer I added, "You know why."

My father threw up his arms in discouragement. "I've done all I could, my boy, to spare you this ordeal. But perhaps it's necessary for you to endure it. You're a man and a soldier. Go, then, where you must go. I ask only that you be brave. In a fortnight, remember, you'll be wearing the uniform of the king."

With that he stepped into the house, leaving me alone on the street, somewhat dizzied by his words and by my sudden freedom. To be brave . . . yes, I felt a sudden confidence in my own powers. My sensitive and sensible father had realized that these were the last hours of my adolescence. A new and more important life was about to begin. My blue artilleryman's uniform would be like a new skin, and in it I should move forward to more glorious things. This prospect was as inebriating as a full-bodied wine. I walked down the Rue de Siam clad in all the gravity of coming of age. By letting me go my father had given me a new sense of responsibility. All my life long I was to remain grateful for the delicacy of feeling he showed on this day.

Yannik was waiting, as he had promised, at the corner. "Not a minute too soon, Little Morgat!" was his greeting. "It doesn't matter, though. We have to wait for the arrival of the second company of the Karrer regiment, which is to be drawn up along the river at the foot of the Castle. I know one of the sergeants, and he'll let us through. I have a good enough reason."

"What's that?"

"To join my father, who's putting the finishing touches on the eight wooden coffins that are needed for . . . after the ceremony."

"Of course," I said mechanically.

"You've got to see them," Yannik added. "The rain goes through the cracks between the boards."

A crowd was gathering on the docks. From the streets of the Seven Saints district clusters of men and women were hurrying toward the Esplanade. The roar of the already assembled multitude swept toward us like the high tide.

"Here are some planks that will do," said Yannik, picking them up from the street and tucking them under my arm, while he piled others across his own shoulder.

Just then the company of the Karrer regiment marched by. The lieutenant in command had a bayonet attached to his gun. Yannik caught sight of his friend the sergeant and signaled to him. Then we fell into line behind the red-coated soldiers. The crowd was reluctant to let them through until they frayed a passage with the butts of their rifles. A woman cursed, but a space opened up and, like a flying wedge, we pushed in.

"The Swiss to the gallows! String them up, too!" the crowd shouted.

After we had passed through and the soldiers had

formed a wall behind us the crowd calmed down. We were in an empty space at the foot of the Castle, whose high walls and towers dominate the mouth of the Penfeld. It was at this spot that I had first caught sight of the beautiful and damned black girl at the prow of the *Rose of Savannah.*

"I know the way," I said to Yannik. "Up the path to the left and around the Castle."

Just then a voice called out behind us, "Where are you going, you two?" The speaker was a soldier on guard at the postern gate.

"We work for Master Maheu, the carpenter, and we're bringing some wood," Yannik explained. "It's for the coffins of Petit-Radet and his men."

"Very good; you can pass," said the soldier, turning his back on us.

From where I stood beside Yannik, we looked out over the Esplanade and the bay. Directly ahead was the brand-new scaffold, topped by a beam with eight ropes wound around it. In the brightening sun the wood shone like gold. Gazing back, I saw the harbor of Brest in all its majesty. Two warships were anchored just offshore; on the foredeck and astride the yards I could see the blue-and-white striped uniforms of the sailors and the officers' dark-blue coats, red breeches and stockings. Farther away the same sight was repeated aboard the frigates and corvettes that were anchored beyond them. Over our heads, in a pine grove, birds were singing.

There was an empty space around the scaffold. Beyond the uniforms—an indistinct medley of reds, whites, and blues—lay the crowd, enveloped in a haze which made it look like a soft and shapeless beast, a giant octopus, whose tentacles were the winding streets which led to the Esplanade and to the sparse trees of the Promenade d'Ajot. I was so overpowered by the inhuman character of the sight that I almost forgot why I was here among these rocks, in this privileged position inside the semicircle which the troops formed in front of the site of the execution.

As far as the eye could see new groups of would-be spectators were converging, in the hope of finding a place. They were condemned, most of them, to see nothing but their neighbors' backs and to hear only the comments of people lucky enough to be standing on stools directly behind the impressive semicircle of soldiers. Toward the Seven Saints district there must have been disturbances, because I saw horsemen of the Royal Cavalry leap into the saddle and scatter over the docks, rousing a storm of protests. Suddenly there was a movement among the standing soldiers. A company of the Karrer regiment lined both sides of a passageway between the postern gate and the six or seven steps leading up to the scaffold. At the foot of a ladder at one side the hangman waited, with his hands behind his back, giving orders to some assistants who were hammering at a block of wood. The magistrates and police of the town took their places in front of the platform. At their right some twenty drummers of the Royal Vessels regiment stood beside their drums, which were stacked in pyramids on the ground.

There was another movement among the troops in front of the scaffold. A subaltern officer approached the drum major and whispered a few words into his ear. The drummers picked up their drums, attached them to their belts and stood still, with their sticks upraised. In the suspenseful silence, broken only by the occasional

call of a sea gull, the postern gate creaked open. The drum major lifted his beribboned baton, whose copper knob was gilded by a ray of sun, and there was a ruffle of drums. My nostrils contracted, my chin quivered, and I felt cold all over. It was all I could do to hold back my tears. A sharp command rang out, bayonets gleamed, and the condemned men, preceded by a priest, emerged from the Castle. Their hands were tied behind their backs and their shoulders bent; they could not resist turning their heads to look at the engine of their destruction. It was all quite natural and yet at the same time unreal. In spite of the heat, I was as if congealed with cold. The loud outcry of the crowd, "There he is!" pierced my ears like a sword.

Now I was all frozen attention; my eyes ached with the strain. I saw exactly what I feared: Mr. Jerome Burns, in the dark-blue coat I knew so well, with half a dozen constables around him. He too walked with stooped shoulders and paused to look up at the ropes hanging from the infernal machine. He grimaced and shrugged his shoulders. I broke into a cold sweat, and my legs started to give way beneath me. Vaguely I heard Yannik's voice say, "Careful, there!" and felt his rough hand grasp my wrist. But my weakness did not last long. I sat down on a rock and looked out to sea, where the *Néère* was outlined against the luminous sky.

The drums kept on rolling.

"That's it! Petit-Radet is swinging!" Yannik exclaimed.

The drums were silent. We walked together down to the harbor. Wishing to be alone, I bade Yannik goodbye. Then, putting the madding crowd behind me, I walked briskly toward "The Anchor of Mercy."

211

20

When I reached home I fell into my father's arms and wept. Striving to overcome his emotion he patted my head and said over and over, "My poor boy! My poor boy!"

My despair was not long-lasting. From that day to this I have seldom wept, and never without good reason.

For some time we did not mention the name that was so much in our thoughts, the name that we chose to remember because he had chosen to give it to us, perhaps as a symbol of his better self. I had been brave, as my father had said I must be, and the victory I won over my own feelings gave me confidence in the future.

I had not many days left now to spend at home. The

open steamer trunk in my room was waiting for me to pack. With the help of Marianne I piled in shoes, stockings, handkerchiefs, wool vests, and linens. The toilet case occupied a place of honor, with a stack of towels on either side to protect it. My uniform—blue with red piping—would be made to order in Metz by the official tailor. Hardly a day passed but that I imagined myself in it. I could see myself in the stagecoach, on my first trip home, bearing myself in a serious and soldierly way. I should get down at the Rue de Siam, and people would whisper, "Isn't that young Morgat, the chandler's son? He's a cadet at the Metz artillery school." A childish fancy, if you like, but one my father and Marianne encouraged as an antidote to my recent sorrow.

I said that we made no mention of Jerome Burns. But we did, eventually, have one last occasion to recall the whole tragic and bloody story. We had just finished our midday dinner, and I was about to go see my friend Nicolas, who was equally busy with preparations for departure, when Pillawer came in, and set his pack down by the door.

"Hello, there!" said my father. "You're just in time for a glass."

"I won't say no to that. What I've seen this morning was enough to curdle my blood."

My father poured a glass of rum, and Pillawer went on with his story.

"I had an appointment to go aboard the *Néère,* to buy some kitchenware that the chief petty officer was authorized to dispose of. They're up at dawn in the King's Navy, I can tell you, and I borrowed a boat from Gadec, the ferryman, to go out to the anchorage. A whole hour I spent arguing with that brass-buttoned bargainer, who

213

wanted to make me pay as much for his discarded pots
and pans as if they were brand-new. When I came ashore
I had the idea of making my way to the Rue de Siam by
the road circling the Castle. As the crow flies, it's the
shortest route. Well, as I came out by the rocks, I saw,
at a distance, the figure of a woman, just at the place
where Trubet was strung up. She seemed, at first, to be
motionless, but suddenly she fell onto her knees and
began to wring her clasped hands as if in desperate
prayer. Then she lowered her head to the ground and
beat her breast repentantly. Poor girl, she was a pitiful
sight! Suddenly, after she had beat her breast again, she
crumpled up, like a flower cut down by the scythe,
and collapsed on the ground, where she lay like a bundle
of rags. I was afraid to go any closer; indeed I didn't
know at all what to do. Several people walking in the
opposite direction, from the docks, seemed equally puz-
zled, for they halted in their tracks and stared at the sight.
When finally they got up their courage to go closer I
followed their example. I was the last to arrive at the
actual scene, just in time to see her dead body, drenched
in blood, taken away. 'But it's Manon! It's Manon de
Gwened!' I shouted. And Manon it was, with a knife
in her bosom, and all the blood run out of her body . . .
Who can fathom the heart of a woman, I ask you? To
see how gaily she used to wait on the tables at the 'Firebrand,' would you ever have thought she'd kill herself
in order to follow a pirate to the grave?"

"That's the last chapter," my father said compassion-
ately. "I believe we can write an end to the story. Yves-
Marie, get your hat and come along with me to buy
something for our supper. I know you were going to see
Nicolas, but I've already invited him to join us this eve-

ning." Pillawer consented to keep the shop in our absence.

"Poor Manon!" I said to my father on the street outside. "What a miserable end she came to! I had an idea, as you may remember, that she was Petit-Radet's mistress . . ."

"Call him Jerome Burns," said my father gently.

"Yes, Jerome Burns's mistress. Quite a girl she was, too . . . But it's all so very strange . . ."

"Manon de Gwened knew one side of him, just as we knew another. It's in the next world, not this, that we can hope to find an explanation."

Dreaming aloud rather than exchanging ideas we walked, like two schoolmates, about the town. At a distance I had a glimpse of the Esplanade, the scene of the hanging. We stopped to refresh ourselves at the "Firebrand" and found it almost deserted. The squadron, which had set sail for an unknown destination the day before, had taken away the officers who were its most faithful devotees. Madame Poder spoke at once of the death of Manon, whom she continued to judge harshly.

It was still light when we came back to "The Anchor of Mercy," and the sign creaked as it swung in the breeze. After a quick upward glance I said, "You really ought to change the shop's name again, Father, and have the sign repainted. It can't stay the way it is now."

My father looked up, in his turn, at Nicolas's handiwork. "Why, Yves-Marie? I see no reason. The man we knew came to cast his last anchor—the anchor of mercy —at our door, and then the storm swept it away. He and the poor wretch dangling at the end of a rope had nothing in common. No, we must leave him his anchor, his last hope, just as we have left him, in spite of everything, a place in our hearts."

So it was that "The Anchor of Mercy" stayed above our door. A few days later, Nicolas and I left Brest together. The excitement of the journey and the prospect of my new uniform made up for the sorrows of leave-taking. Soon Nicolas's high spirits put an end to my moment of melancholy.

Nicolas rode into Paris like a Spanish conquistador entering a town of Peru. Even after his initial self-confidence had been taken down a peg he continued to believe in his lucky star. One of his cousins, who belonged to the French Guards, showed us the city. Alas, I could stay only three days, until the departure of the stagecoach for Metz.

Nicolas took me to the stage. It was filled to capacity, but I was lucky enough to have a corner seat, where I managed to snatch some sleep; an artillery officer, who seemed to me a harbinger of good luck, was my neighbor. At Châlons-sur-Marne we lost many passengers, and after the last change of horses I was able to stretch myself out quite comfortably.

We arrived at Metz very late at night. The stage rumbled loudly over the paving stones, and the houses on either side of the street seemed higher than those to which I was accustomed. But in the darkness everything had such a fantastic appearance that I could not trust my own eyes, even if I kept them wide open. We came to a halt in the courtyard of an inn, where a stable boy was holding up a huge lantern.

"Are you Yves-Marie Morgat?"

A priest from the school was waiting for me. As far as I could make out in the yellow light cast by the lantern he was a gaunt man with a nose like that of an albatross. He gave orders to a stout young fellow sprawling in a wheelbarrow, who proceeded to unload my trunk and then to trundle it along. Ten minutes later a gate, ornamented with heraldic bearings, swung open in a high wall. A bell tinkled and our footsteps echoed in what seemed like an interminable hall.

Such was my entry into the Royal Artillery School of Metz. I shall say nothing of my stay there, except that it was attended by a host of minor annoyances and considerable unhappiness. At this time the military schools' requirement of noble birth was in the process of modification. Most of the cadets came from the Collège des Quatre-Nations, founded by Cardinal Mazarin for the benefit of the sons of penniless noblemen. But because there were not enough artillerymen to carry on the imminent war the regulations were relaxed and some middle-class boys, myself among them, were admitted. I was a cadet, to be sure, but one who was made to feel that he was not quite "top drawer." My future prospects were none too bright.

Thanks, however, to hard work and to a certain facility in mathematics, geography, and letters, I found a place as a second lieutenant in the Navy Bombardiers. My hat was not a tricorn but a mitre, and I went to sea almost immediately aboard the frigate *La Radieuse*.

At just this time my father died and, for want of anyone to carry on the business, "The Anchor of Mercy" was sold. The new owners lost little time in tearing it down and building a house of quite a different character. I was at sea, and hence I could not save the sign that had hung over the door. It was buried, along with my youth, amid the fallen plaster.